THE FANTASTIC
ADVENTURES OF

Captain Acorn

AVALON ROBINSON

Printed in the United States of America

First Printing, 2018

ISBN: 978-0-9600825-0-6

For Mommy, who called me an author when I begged to differ and had the highest of standards for my humor.

Romans 15:13

TABLE OF CONTENTS

CHAPTER ONE
A SQUIRREL IS NAMED,
A CREW IS CHOSEN

The family was driving in the car when something happened. It was not an extraordinary thing. It also wasn't necessarily a special thing. If I'm being entirely truthful, it was a thing that has happened to many, many families. The fact of the matter is that this particular family were all driving in the car when it happened: a stuffed animal was held up in the backseat, named, and a story unfolded.

The stuffed animal in question was a small squirrel, smaller than the father's hand on the steering wheel of the car. The squirrel itself was a caramel brown color with a creamy belly. It had short but soft fabric for fur, except for its tail which was much fuller and seemed almost the same size as the animal itself. Its whiskers were made from a rather droopy floss that curved around its mouth rather than extending stiff and proud. Finally, the squirrel's eyes and nose were black and quite literally beady.

When the squirrel was held aloft, it was in a moment of triumph from having finally settled on a name. The squirrel belonged to the youngest of the four girls in the family. She and her sisters had been trying to name the squirrel for some time, but nothing had felt particularly right until the youngest tested out the name Acorn. That name held real promise to her and so she explored it further. To her, it seemed that Acorn wasn't good enough as a name on its own. She considered what she could do to fix that situation and the best solution seemed to be adding "Captain" to the name. There never was much known about how Acorn became a captain, but it was agreed that the squirrel was very much suited to the name: Captain Acorn. From there, only one more thing was necessary for Captain Acorn. She needed a story. Thankfully a story was all too willing to begin.

Captain Acorn was setting out on a voyage. This was not unusual, as the sisters soon decided that Captain Acorn wasn't just a captain, but a well-known one at that. In fact, when they started their story, Captain Acorn was already so well known and liked that other animals would jostle and push each other at stadium auditions just to join her crew. As this was discussed by the sisters, the adults laughed openly from the front seat of the car. The children didn't mind it so much and saw the humor in it. It was a little silly, I suppose, that a single squirrel could become so popular that she would fill a stadium, but that was just Captain Acorn's way.

So in this stadium packed full of eager animals, the air was thick with excitement and anxiety. Excitement, because each of them felt that wild flicker of hope that their application could be chosen out of the thousands, and anxiety because they knew just how steep those odds were. Fortunately, when the music started, the smoke machine started going, and the stage started rising, all fears were completely forgotten in the wild cries of excitement.

This may seem like a pretty ridiculous way to start the event, but for Acorn it was just right. You see, she was a very theatrical squirrel. When you have a stadium available to you for your own purposes, you can make as dramatic of an entrance as you want to, which is exactly what Acorn was doing. The crowd roared and whooped with excitement as the small squirrel burst through the haze, waving with one paw and giving a little salute to the crowd with the other. When she reached the microphone at the far end of the stage, she waved a few more times. Several animals felt sure that she had waved directly at them and could hardly believe their luck. After a few more minutes of enjoying the attention probably too much, Acorn raised her paws for silence and a hush fell over the crowd.

"Ladies and gentlemen!" Acorn began after a long pause. "You are here today to hear the crew results for my latest voyage. I want to say first that I'm very impressed with the applications this time. There were so many wonderful, fine applicants and I wish I could take you all with me!"

The crowd cheered enthusiastically at this, each feeling momentarily comforted by the idea that she had liked them all so well.

"But!" Captain Acorn continued, and her voice became much more serious which made all the creatures suddenly regret thinking they were so well liked. "I only have so many slots available. Still," And she looked out warmly at all the eager animals who leaned forward in their seats, "I hope that even if you aren't chosen today, you won't give up on your dream of sailing and keep coming back!"

The animals cheered again, feeling a little encouraged by her words. They now felt ready to face the outcome of Acorn's selection. Sensing this, Acorn motioned offstage to her only permanent crew member.

Acorn always kept the same First Mate. The title had long ago gone to her oldest and most loyal companion, a small cream colored cat with tan paws named Pounce. Acorn had considered making more official and permanent positions available on her crew. Unfortunately, the four young sisters who had named her knew very little about life aboard a ship and had to pretend that first mate was the only other available position with a title beyond "crew".

Acorn and Pounce were in many ways very close friends, but Acorn would never admit it so openly. It seemed Acorn had this sort of idea that she couldn't be too chummy with her crew, even if she was incredibly fond of them. Which – in Pounce's case – she was. Pounce never minded though, and openly called Acorn her friend all the time. This sometimes rubbed Acorn the wrong way and she would try to act like she didn't really need a friend (even though she definitely did).

Pounce walked onstage nowhere near as dramatically as Acorn. While she was a very high energy cat, she was a little crowd shy and didn't get the same thrill out of having thousands of animals looking at her that Acorn got. She carefully brought forward a giant envelope, placed it in Acorns paws, and then stepped back just far enough so that she was out of the exact spotlight. She immediately felt much more comfortable.

Captain Acorn, on the other hand, was loving every moment of being in the spotlight. Every animal leaned forward on their seat as she broke the seal of the envelope. One rabbit leaned so far forward that he fell off his seat and had to scramble back up in a hurry. He hoped Acorn hadn't seen it, but since he was in a very distant seat and could only see what was happening by looking at the large screen over the stage, it seemed likely that his clumsiness had gone unnoticed.

Just when it seemed like the stadium couldn't get any quieter, Acorn cleared her throat and spoke. "I will now begin announcing the crew for my latest voyage aboard my world famous ship: the Golden Acorn!"

Every animal found a way to lean in even further as Captain Acorn slid the paper out of the envelope and read the first name there.

"Theodore Froglen!"

The stadium erupted into noise. It wasn't necessarily cheers and whoops of excitement. In fact, every animal who wasn't Theodore Froglen felt a little whoosh of fear, disappointment, and jealousy that their name wasn't the one called. Still, most felt very confident that their own name would eventually be called, and they wanted that moment to be as perfect as it could be. So, they cheered less out of happiness for Mr. Froglen, and more out of the thinking that if they cheered for him, everyone else would be compelled to cheer for them when their name was called.

The Theodore Froglen in question was a lanky little frog who was so shocked at hearing his name called that he could barely stand and walk down to the stage. But stand and walk he did, and when he had shaken hands with Captain Acorn herself, he was shown the way backstage to wait till the end of the show when all the crew would be brought onstage to take a bow.

The noise quickly died down again and Acorn read the next name on the list.

"Jacob Crockey!"

The polite cheering erupted again and this time a crocodile with a rather uncomfortably large smile made his way confidently to the stage in the same way that Froglen had. This naming went on for the next hour or so, Acorn always shouting the name dramatically into the microphone, the crowd always cheering to be polite, and the stunned animal walking up to the stage while it could hardly believe its good luck. Bears, lizards, birds, rabbits, and a wide variety of other animals were called one by one to the stage. Even the little rabbit who had fallen off his seat was called down second to last.

Eventually, though, the last name was called and all the other animals had to deal with the disappointment that they would have to apply again next year. For the animals that had been chosen, though, they went to sleep that night hardly able to breathe from all the excitement of knowing they were about to set sail with the world famous Captain Acorn.

The next morning, the newly appointed crew was all waiting eagerly in the harbor to set out. They stretched their necks and peered around corners as they made their way through the harbor until at last one excited rabbit cried.

"There it is! There SHE is!" Whether this rabbit was referring to the ship or Acorn itself is hard to say, mainly because of general amazement at both.

The Golden Acorn was the product of the youngest sister imagining that Captain Acorn deserved the very best ship for adventuring, and the best ship seemed to her to be a fantastically large galleon, which was a type of ship she had learned about in school when discussing the Age of Exploration. Captain Acorn's adventures seemed as good a place as any to put that knowledge to use, and so that's what the ship was.

The sails and masts and rails and ropes and decks all awed the animals waiting on the docks. But more striking than any of that was seeing Captain

Acorn standing at the helm and looking down at them. Any fears the crew had about going to sea vanished at the sight of that noble squirrel watching the open ocean beyond the harbor. How could they go wrong following that squirrel? She was looking so fearlessly at the sea, they felt that they were unstoppable with her at the helm. They all settled into their bunks at lightning speed with a new excitement in their hearts.

It's probably for the best that they never knew that Captain Acorn was at that moment staring into the distance with so much intensity because she was trying to remember if she had left the stove on back at her house before she left. This shouldn't be counted against her, though. As I've said, she was a very fearless squirrel and the odds are that if she hadn't been wondering about the stove, she would have been staring off into the distance anyway. So really, it counts either way.

CHAPTER TWO
CAPTAIN ACORN ATTENDS A PARTY

It's a simple truth that being a famous captain of a very famous ship means people will want you to do things and be places. Sometimes, people who encounter this kind of attention get extremely nervous by having so much focus on them and look for ways to avoid it at all costs. There are others, of course, who find the attention very appealing and actively seek it out to some degree. Squirrels tend to be the second kind of person, and Captain Acorn was no different.

She knew that her celebrity status brought plenty of attention her way. Her first love was the sea, but her second love was getting attention. Fortunately for her, these two things very often went hand in hand with each other. When she was on her voyages, she often made a point of visiting places where she was extra well known and liked for her adventures. Pounce was tremendously understanding of this need for attention and believed that it was best for her Captain's health if they put ashore every once and a while to give Acorn just that. It was an excellent arrangement in that Pounce always announced these ports to the crew so that Acorn could act surprised when she went ashore as though she had no idea she was so well liked there, and declare "My isn't it embarrassing to get so much attention?"

It was at one such port when Captain Acorn got the opportunity for even more admiration. After a few weeks of uneventful open sea, the crew of the Golden Acorn spotted land and made for it. It wasn't a surprising speck of land. The land in question was a well-known island nation simply called Bunny Island.

The bunnies of Bunny Island were not your typical rabbit. When the parents in the front seat of the car briefly interrupted to ask what kind of rabbits they were, the children only said that they were fancy rabbits, assuming that this was more than enough explanation for the adult mind. In many ways it was. When I think of the word "fancy," I think of expensive clothing, houses with lots of marble in them, and gadgets and knick-knacks that make sense to the people who own them but only confuse guests. The rabbits of Bunny Island were all these things and then some. They liked nice things but shared generously with anyone who came to their island, making it a very popular tourist destination for those willing to make the voyage.

Acorn liked this island in particular, not only for its appreciation of finer things but also because they generally adored her. This might be because she and Pounce once helped them with a particularly bad problem in which a band of pirates continually attacked their shores, stealing jewels, spray painting houses, and mismatching everyone's socks. Since then, the residents of Bunny Island were always hugely excited to see the Golden Acorn pull into their harbor.

While Acorn was waving down to all the eager rabbits on the dock below, Pounce was happily pulling the mail sack up the side of the ship, feeling very glad that the First Mate wasn't expected to be so popular and good with people. Pounce could, in a moment of pure happiness, often find herself in the center of attention, but there is a very large difference between wanting to be the center of attention and finding yourself the center of attention. Occasions on which Pounce found herself being the center of attention were usually accidental and resulted from her getting too excited about something. She didn't seek it out, and she was more than happy to point focus towards her captain. This was something Captain Acorn particularly appreciated about her First Mate, it's difficult to stir up praise for yourself single-handedly, but it's even harder to compete for it. On both, these matters Pounce was a huge help to Acorn.

As Pounce sorted through the mail, she found at the top of the stack a large golden envelope with Captain Acorn's name on it and a return address that was from the Bunny Island presidential palace. Knowing this was something her captain would want right away, she brought it over to Acorn and placed it in her paw with enough of a flourish that the crowd below could see it.

Acorn greatly appreciated the flourish and, in the same dramatic, flourishing way, opened up the envelope and read it to herself. Ordinarily, it is very rude to stop interacting with someone, or in this case, a lot of someones to read a message. This was an exception, however, as all the bunnies below recognized exactly where the letter was from and they waited eagerly to see what Captain Acorn would say. After reading for a moment longer, Captain Acorn smiled down on all the animals below and called out:

"My good rabbits of Bunny Island! I would be very honored to attend your gala! I'm very excited to spend the day with such wonderful rabbits. I will see you all at the gala this evening!"

The rabbits on the dock all cheered wildly and immediately left to get themselves ready, all save a few young rabbits who stayed staring up at the Golden Acorn because they thought that the ship was much more entertaining and thrilling than any party.

That night, Acorn, Pounce, and a large selection of the crew all made their way to the Presidential Palace for the gala. The Bunny Islanders held many balls in a year, but this was the first time they had thrown a gala and they couldn't believe their luck that Captain Acorn had come to visit just then. The whole reason they were throwing a gala, was because the oldest sister had learned that word in her vocabulary lesson that week and had been searching for an opportunity to try it out.

The Bunny Island presidential palace was an extremely beautiful place. The members of Acorn's crew who hadn't ever done much traveling stared in awe at everything they saw, while the ones who had some traveling experience tried to look as though they had seen nicer things before. Acorn had a very steady reaction to the palace, but that was largely because she had been there before. Pounce had been there too but was so excited to be back you might have thought it was her first time there. Acorn tried to stay dignified while her first mate bounced back and forth, almost shaking from excitement. Once or twice she had to whisper "Pounce, please." through her smile, and that would check Pounce, if only for a moment.

The only other crew member to have a dignified reaction to the palace was Margaret Bunnerton, who was walking on Captain Acorn's left. Bunnerton came from a long line of rabbits from Bunny Island and was part of a well to do family. The only reason she didn't live there now was that she had moved to the mainland to continue her education in sailing and apply for a position on Captain Acorn's crew. During her childhood, she had been to many balls at the Presidential Palace with her parents and had learned every piece of rabbit etiquette there is to know. This was the main reason Acorn was keeping her close by at the gala, besides finding her company very enjoyable.

Bunnerton was being extremely helpful as they entered the grand ballroom, quietly whispering instructions for the rest of the crew, who weren't as familiar with Bunny Island customs, to hold still and wait while they were all announced. A very stuffy, old rabbit soon tapped his cane for attention and all the bunnies in the ballroom turned their attention to the entrance while he announced: "Ladies and Gentleman, the crew of the Golden Acorn, lead by the great and wonderful Captain Acorn herself. Accompanied by First Mate Pounce, and Bunny Island's very own Margaret Bunnerton."

Bunnerton whispered a little "oh my!" to herself, having not expected to be announced alongside her captain, and looked a little embarrassed over at Acorn. But Acorn merely gave a polite nod and smiled warmly at her crew member. Acorn was so confident in the attention she received that she didn't mind having a moment of it go to a well deserving crew member.

With a little blush, Bunnerton gestured the way into the main part of the ballroom, allowing Acorn to go first and followed behind. The only thing that threatened to distract her was looking for her parents, who she knew would be in the crowd of bunnies and who were incredibly proud of their young daughter for her early success. She eventually spotted them near the ice sculpture and gave the smallest, shy wave she could manage in response to their big, excited one.

For her part, Acorn was already swimming in attention from the important rabbits of the island. Bunnerton whispered in Acorn's ear which important rabbit was which just before they reached them so that Acorn was always prepared to greet them with a smile and a nod by name. A squirrel as important as Acorn was used to meeting and greeting a thousand different important animals whenever she was in port, and she thrived on the ceremony of it all. For their part, the important rabbits all came away from meeting Acorn feeling deeply impressed by the squirrel who already knew their names and customs and they all nodded amongst themselves and said things like: "You see why she has such a fantastic reputation with extraordinary manners like that!"

About thirty minutes after Acorn and the crew had arrived, the president of Bunny Island appeared on a balcony high above the ballroom. President Fluffton was a very old but very respected rabbit. During his time in office, he had made good on a promise to bring better education about cutlery etiquette to the island. He raised a frail old paw to quiet the happy but dignified cheering and then made a few remarks about the wonderful turnout, honored guests (and here he made a polite nod in Acorn's direction that did not go unnoticed), and declared that the dancing would now start.

Several members of Captain Acorn's crew suddenly found themselves very disappointed by the gala and wished that they had stayed on board the ship where there was a small, wild party taking place. They had been expecting a bit more of a celebration and were met instead with very serious, formal dancing.

The Bunny Islanders were not overly concerned with upbeat music and generally preferred tunes that sounded to the crew like stiff, boring music you would hear in an elevator. These rabbits liked finer things, as I've said before, and most of them had received very formal, very classical dance training in their childhood and liked to pull it out for the social events on the island.

To the crew members of the Golden Acorn who were not familiar with these rather intricate dances that relied on knowing a complicated series of steps ahead of time, the gala was now a huge disappointment. Jacob Crockey, in particular, made sure everyone near him knew that he didn't like the party anymore. He was a grumpy crocodile who was rarely pleased with anything and was always trying to make sure that someone else was grumpy with him.

"Great party," he muttered sarcastically to an uncomfortable looking young rabbit standing nearby. "I'm definitely glad I got dressed up for this. It's not like I didn't have anything else that I would have rather been doing."

Acorn glared angrily at him as she walked past and Crockey switched from talking about being disappointed to looking disappointed, which is not as effective but still gets your point across. Acorn, Pounce, Bunnerton, and a few other crew members were familiar with these dances and fell into the steps without any hesitation whenever a partner became available. For Acorn there was constantly the issue of availability, but the opposite. Every rabbit there wanted to dance with the famous Captain Acorn and every rabbit tried. She was a gracious squirrel in these situations with impeccable manners, so everyone who asked her was given the opportunity for a dance. For the most part, these dances were second nature to her, and nothing special. It wasn't until around eleven that the gala escalated in ways Acorn had not been anticipating.

A particularly intricate dance had just ended and as the animals all applauded politely towards the orchestra, an incredibly tall, handsome rabbit approached Acorn. If it had been Pounce or Bunnerton in this situation, they would have either become incredibly embarrassed or fled into the crowd.

Acorn, however, was a very confident squirrel who wasn't easily intimidated, so this attention was not only welcome but not frightening either. When he made a flourishing bow and asked: "May I have this dance?" Acorn accepted without hesitation or shyness.

"I'm Charles Hopper," the rabbit said smoothly as he whisked Acorn away across the dance floor. The band was playing a well-known waltz that Acorn and her partner easily fell into. Ordinarily, Acorn would have returned the introduction. She was so well known at this gala, however, that she hardly thought it necessary and instead coyly replied.

"It's a pleasure to meet you, Mr. Hopper. You are an excellent dance partner." Most of the time Acorn said this to make a dance partner feel less nervous about dancing with her so they wouldn't step on her paws so often but with Mr. Hopper, she genuinely meant the compliment. He was a fantastic dancer and you could tell that he had taken his dance education very seriously from a young age. Acorn wished that more animals took care to keep the practice of finer arts in top condition. If they did, she would have more to talk about with people. Still, Mr. Hopper seemed up to the challenge so she pursued the topic by complimenting him. Acorn was a witty and clever squirrel and had learned a long time ago that you can make someone think you are a brilliant conversationalist by getting them to talk about themselves. Mr. Hopper surprised her, however.

"You are very kind," He returned. He smiled through his attractively large two front teeth and twitched his long brown ears good-naturedly. "Though I think my dancing is largely thanks to having such an excellent partner. I can tell you've been classically trained. May I ask what school?"

"Thank you!" Captain Acorn said, almost a little too enthusiastically. As you can imagine, Acorn was of a very small population that actually found conversations about classical training and dance technique and etiquette interesting. She had tried in the past to explain the complicated workings of it all to Pounce, but every time she turned around from her presentation slides she found her first mate fast asleep, or completely distracted and not paying any attention. She had tried to find different methods of presenting the material to Pounce, but ultimately learned it wasn't how she was presenting it. Pounce just found the whole subject incredibly boring.

Even Bunnerton had found it difficult to keep up with Acorn's dedication to the rules and etiquette of formal dancing. While she had learned all the rules in her childhood on Bunny Island and knew them by heart to this day, she didn't share Acorn's enthusiasm for discussing them, which gives some clues to why she had gone to school on the mainland. In Bunnerton's defense, we can't be expected to embrace every tradition we are raised with or we would never have any room to grow and make our own.

For their part, the sisters in the car knew that Captain Acorn cared about these things but didn't actually known them themselves. All they knew was that they were deeply complex. The oldest sister had tried to explain it to the others, but after a few minutes, the other three had realized that she was just making it up and she became too embarrassed to keep up the act.

In the interest of not becoming as bored as poor Pounce and Bunnerton in those instances, I will say that Mr. Hopper and Captain Acorn spent the next three waltzes talking excitedly about etiquette and enjoying each other's company more and more. Every time they passed Pounce at the buffet table the two seemed more and more like old friends and Pounce couldn't help but notice that Acorn was acting less like the formal captain she always portrayed and more like the very particular squirrel that she played board games in the captain's cabin with a few evenings a week. Unfortunately, things that seem to be going very well don't always stay going very well.

Just as a lively foxtrot was starting, a short, round hamster walked up to Captain Acorn and made a stiff, deep bow.

"Captain Acorn," he said briskly, "My name is Captain Hamsterton. I was wondering if I could have a word with you."

It's not that Captain Hamsterton's request itself was rude, but he had just seriously breached a rule of Bunny Island dance etiquette that roughly stated that non-dancing conversation shouldn't interrupt a dance after it's already started. Hamsterton didn't seem like the kind of animal that was particularly in the know about such a rule, though, so Captain Acorn was willing to forgive.

"Of course," Acorn said politely, but not as friendly as she had been talking with Mr. Hopper. "A dance just started though, so I will have to-"

"Excellent!" chirped Captain Hamsterton. It would seem that he hadn't taken any notice that Acorn wasn't actually immediately agreeing to the conversation, or perhaps he didn't want to acknowledge that, which is a much worse thing to do. "I have several points to speak to you about. First about us combining our forces in sailing. Second-"

"Mr. Hamsterton," Acorn said coldly. Around her, other animals had stopped dancing to watch what was happening more closely. Pounce had even edged away from the food to better hear what was going on. "I will be able to speak with you in a moment, but not right now. And I don't particularly appreciate you interrupting me."

Now it was Hamsterton's turn to grow cold. He scrunched his nose angrily and rose up in height, which wasn't really all that impressive since he was a round, short hamster, but it made him feel better about the situation. "It's not Mr. Hamsterton," he said through his scrunched nose, "It's *Captain* Hamsterton. Should I presume, then, that you don't want to discuss our partnership?"

"I can't see that I would particularly benefit from it." Acorn shrugged, and Mr. Hopper let out a small laugh from behind her.

Hamsterton sneered and looked into Captain Acorn's eyes with his own beady ones. "Interesting," he said quietly.

"What is interesting?" Acorn asked a little more calmly than she actually felt. On any other occasion, she would have already requested a duel for the interruption, but this was a very fancy gala and she was trying to keep the evening civil.

"Well," sneered Hamsterson, "It's just that I would have expected a bigger squirrel for such a massive ego."

The effect of the insult was instantaneous. Acorn went as pale as a furry squirrel can and Mr. Hopper suddenly clenched his paws into fists. Anyone who was standing near enough to hear what was said gave a loud gasp. Several animals who hadn't been near enough to listen gasped anyway so they weren't left out, and animals who heard all the gasping suddenly turned their attention towards the center of the room, hoping to catch on to what all the commotion was about.

"What are you suggesting?" Acorn hissed between her clenched teeth. She knew herself exactly what was being suggested, but she was a very rational squirrel and would have preferred that Hamsterton be the attacker so that when she responded she could keep the goodwill of the Bunny Islanders.

"Now, now Acorn," Hamsterton sneered meanly, "Best not to get short with each other."

If nothing had been done, it's very likely that a duel would have happened right then and there. This would have been incredibly unfortunate as they are not typically a part of a gala and would have ruined the whole mood of the evening. In the end, Bunnerton proved to be the most useful in this situation. She suddenly stepped forward, wrinkling her nose cautiously at all the tension in the room and stood between her furious captain and the insulting hamster with two presidential palace guards entering the scene behind her. It would seem that while other animals were eagerly watching the fight unfold, Bunnerton had done something diplomatic about it.

As with most animals in this situation, the moment it became clear to Hamsterton that his actions were getting dangerously close to having consequences he began to bluster nervously and tried his best to act like the whole incident was no big deal. No one else said anything or moved, but Hamsterton quickly saw that the room respected Acorn far more than him and had taken her side.

"Hamsters!" He called out as regally as he could, and several hamsters from different points around the room poked their heads out of the crowd. "We must be returning to the ship!" He turned to face where the president was sitting. "Thank you for your kind hospitality, sir. I look forward to joining the people of Bunny Island at a future gala."

Most people in the room didn't feel so sure that Hamsterton would ever be welcomed back. Before he could leave, he looked Acorn in the eye again and said only loud enough for those closest to hear: "I won't be forgetting your snub or your manners in a hurry, Acorn."

It probably would have been best if Acorn had let Hamsterton's humiliation be enough punishment for him. At any rate, that would have been the more polite thing to do. Acorn was still feeling incredibly insulted, however, and this last remark felt like too much, so it's not all that surprising that before Hamsterton could disappear into the crowd she stepped forward past Bunnerton and Pounce.

"It's interesting that you would choose to insult me with remarks about shortness." Captain Acorn observed, "When you seem to be short in every sense of the word. Short of class, dignity, respect for your fellow animal, and not least of all stature."

A low murmur ran through the crowd. Some animals seemed to disapprove of Acorn giving an insult back while others were visibly trying their hardest not to laugh openly, having appreciated the joke. For his part, Hamsterton glared furiously at her and then turned on his heel and marched out of the palace with his hamster crew in tow.

With a few more murmurs the party slowly resumed. Acorn continued dancing with Mr. Hopper and other dignified guests but the enjoyment had been largely taken out of the evening. So most of the crew, especially the ones who hadn't been enjoying the gala in the first place, were greatly relieved when after only a little while longer she signaled for them to prepare to leave and made her very polite remarks to the president and other important rabbits.

The mood was more than a little sour as the crew walked back through the empty streets to the harbor. Acorn still felt furious and wasn't doing the best job hiding it.

"You know, Captain," Bunnerton said unexpectedly in the silence. "I think we learned something amazing about the bunnies here tonight."

"What's that?" Said Acorn in a glum voice that meant she wasn't actually all that interested.

"We Bunny Islanders don't make a habit of picking sides." Bunnerton said thoughtfully, "It's how we've stayed out of just about every major war. I always thought we never would. But for the first time tonight, I saw Bunny Islanders pick a side, and they chose you. That is a great honor."

Acorn smiled warmly at Bunnerton. She had the distinct feeling that the rabbit was saying most of this just to cheer her up, but she didn't care because it was working. Maybe she really was just that great of a squirrel after all.

"Thank you Bunnerton," she said kindly, "and thank you for everything you did tonight."

"I would have been right behind her, captain!" Pounce promised eagerly, bouncing up unexpectedly from behind "It's just that I had just had a huge bite of cake and I remembered what you said about talking with my mouth full at fancy places and I was trying to chew as fast as I could."

That night as Acorn fell asleep in her own cabin on her own ship where she was respected and admired, she decided that some things were much nicer than a fancy gala.

CHAPTER THREE
THE GOLDEN ACORN MEETS A STORM

As I've said, the sisters never gave much thought to how Captain Acorn became a captain, but they were always very sure that her experience spoke for itself. This was probably a large reason why Acorn was such a confident squirrel. Even confident squirrels are sometimes given a bit of trouble, though, but that usually takes something extraordinarily large. It had been years since Acorn had run into an extraordinarily large challenge, so it worked out that, in a lot of ways, she was due for one.

One day Captain Acorn was in her cabin reading. She always took several books along with her on any voyage. Her mother had once told her that a well-read squirrel was a smart squirrel, and Acorn knew you have to be a very smart squirrel to survive out on the open sea. She had just finished rereading "Practical Knots for the Seafaring Squirrel" and was starting on "Back to the Rabbit Hole", which was supposedly a very sad story about two rabbits trying to find each other after years of being apart. Acorn didn't like the idea of reading it, but Bunnerton had recommended it to her and she didn't want to seem like she couldn't handle a sad story.

"Besides!" she thought to herself as she opened the book, "I'm one of the toughest squirrels out there! I'm not going to let some book make me cry!"

About an hour later, there was a knock on her cabin door.

"Enter!" She called, quickly wiping her eyes.

Pounce entered with Froglen behind her. The cat opened her mouth to ask one question, but when she saw her captain's puffy eyes asked instead "Captain? Have you been crying?"

"No! Nonsense! What a ridiculous idea!" Said Acorn in a way that said, "Oh my goodness, yes I have! This is the saddest book I've ever read!"

Pounce and Froglen looked at each other curiously, and Acorn could see that she was in danger of being doubted, which was her least favorite thing behind being ignored, so she quickly said: "State your business, Pounce! I have a very important, practical book to get back to."

"Well, Captain." Said Pounce, "It's Froglen. He was on lookout duty just now and well-"

"Storm clouds, Captain," Froglen said. He knew it was impolite to interrupt someone as important as the First Mate, but this was his first time having a meeting in the Captain's cabin and he was a little excited, so he should be forgiven. "At least, I think so, Captain. I'm not as experienced a sailor, so I thought maybe you would want to look at them, just to be sure."

Acorn gave a short nod, glad that the attention was away from her reading and on something tougher. "Well done, Mr. Froglen. That is an excellent idea."

Froglen might have fainted from the excitement of being told "well done" by such an important squirrel if Acorn hadn't immediately strolled out on deck and he didn't need to scramble after her and Pounce to keep up.

The crew of the Golden Acorn was already looking nervously away to the East, and Acorn could immediately see why. Large, dark storm clouds were moving quickly towards them and the sea in front of those clouds seemed like it was already rocking to and fro with massive waves and beating rain. The sails of the Golden Acorn were already flapping wildly in the wind and the crew kept switching back and forth between looking worriedly at the ship and looking nervously at the storm.

"Spyglass, please," Acorn said calmly, and Pounce scrambled to get it for her. Acorn was a clever squirrel and understood that if she stayed calm, the crew would stay calm as well. It is rather admirable that she could face a massive storm with an entirely relaxed face while her mind was saying "oh no, oh no" on a very steady, very nervous loop. She had learned long ago though, that calmness is very rarely for just yourself. Most of the time, when you need to be calm most is when other people are looking at you for what to do. It's ten times easier to be calm for someone else than it is for just yourself, and Acorn very wisely saw that the whole crew would benefit more from her being calm than visibly scared. Still, when Pounce returned with her spyglass, she took a closer look at the storm and the "oh no"s in her mind got louder and faster. The waves were indeed absolutely massive and the rain was thick and angry.

"Pounce," Acorn said still calmly, "I believe a rather large storm is indeed about to hit us. Please ready the crew."

"Yes, Captain." Pounce said. She would have sounded just as calm as Acorn if her voice hadn't suddenly become alarmingly high and squeaky.

The crew all rushed about the ship making it ready to face the storm and responding to any order Acorn or Pounce called out. These orders were largely gibberish and made very little sense. It was less an issue of lacking preparedness on Acorn's part, and more an issue of the sisters playing. They knew very little about sailing and so they could only give commands that they had heard used before. Most of them outright contradicted each other, which made it hard for the parents not to laugh, but somehow Acorn was still fully in control of the ship and felt ready to face the storm in about five minutes flat. This was an extraordinarily good thing because, as it turns out, the storm was ready to hit them in about five and a half minutes.

Acorn enjoyed almost every single part of sailing, but like any sensible captain, she absolutely despised storms. She didn't mind watching them when she was onshore in her cozy, seaside penthouse and could hold a warm cup of coffee in her paws and see the lightning from a great distance. In a lot of ways, she rather liked to see them. Out at sea, though, storms took on an entirely different nature. They were loud and dangerous, and they had a nasty habit of battering her beloved ship within an inch of its' life and Acorn had no love for anything that harmed her beloved Golden Acorn. So just before the storm hit, she shook her paw in a rage and then all at once the storm responded.

With a tremendous roll of thunder and a flash of lightning that was uncomfortably close to the ship, the storm began attacking the Golden Acorn and its crew. The ship tilted dangerously to one side as a stormy wave pounded against it and the vast majority of the crew, who didn't know what to do in a storm at sea, slid across the wet deck and landed in a pile on the other side. A few crew members would have been swept overboard if Acorn, who was no beginner when it came to storms, hadn't grabbed them by their tails, feathers, or whatever else she could grab and held on tight. The ship soon righted itself again, but it was a temporary solution to a very big problem.

The rain was coming down so hard and so fast that Acorn was having trouble seeing anything clearly. She tried wiping the rain from her eyes with her paw, but was soaked again the next second. Still, she knew she needed to get to work if she was going to save her ship and she stumbled up to the helm where Pounce was struggling to keep the ship under control.

"A bit stormy out!" Pounce shouted when Acorn joined her.

"Pounce, you know I enjoy a good joke as much as the next squirrel, but right now really isn't the time." Acorn bellowed back.

Acorn was very right about that. Pounce's joke did nothing to lessen the storm and that was still the most pressing problem. The ship itself was doing well as the crew worked frantically, even if all the animals looked extremely seasick. That's to be expected though when one moment you are sailing up a wave the size of a mountain and then next you are plunging down the other side. For the most part, the animals were learning to keep their paws steady on the deck, even if there was still a lot of slipping going on in the rain. The thunder and lighting made it hard to see or do anything, but the animals were trying their best to keep the ship steady and it was starting to look like their best was going to be enough.

Only one problem remained. The second sister remembered that old ships in storms always needed to wrap up their sails in a certain way so that all the wind from the storm wasn't pushing the ship around too fast. At the moment, the Golden Acorn's sails were full of storm-wind and it was pushing the ship into the massive waves much faster than was safe by Captain Acorn standards. Acorn saw this as the most pressing need at the moment and started yelling orders through all the noise of the storm.

"All animals! Bring those sails in! Quickly!"

Not every animal heard her through all the thunder and wind, but enough crew members started scrambling to bring the sails in that she was satisfied that the job was getting done. As each sail was brought in, the ship seemed to get a little steadier and slowed down a little bit. Despite the noise and rain, Acorn was actually starting to think that maybe the storm wasn't going to be too hard on her ship after all. Of course, the moment you start to think like that is usually when one more disaster likes to strike, which is exactly what happened to Acorn.

The last and biggest sail was just about to be taken in when Bunnerton suddenly gave a loud shout of dismay that immediately caught Acorn's attention. The rope needed to secure the sail was soaked through by the rain and it had slipped right between Bunnerton's paws. Now it was flapping wildly in the wind and no one on the deck could grab it. Like a good captain, Acorn took in the whole situation, not just the problem of the rope. She looked at the sea around her to see how much of a problem it would be to have the last sail down. There she saw a massive wave, bigger than any the storm brought so far, headed straight for them. Worse yet, the wind was pushing them into it sideways. If the wave hit them like that, it would swallow the ship and that would be the end of Captain Acorn and her crew.

Acorn looked around frantically for a crew member who could get to the rope without needing to climb to it. There were a couple of birds on her crew, but she worried that with their wings they would be easily carried off by the storm winds and she wasn't about to lose any members of her crew. She needed a leaper, and her eyes fell on Theodore Froglen.

"Mr. Froglen!" She called and he hopped over to her in a single bound as the ship rocked to and fro. "Mr. Froglen, can you make the jump to that rope?"

Now, almost everyone in the world struggles with fear occasionally, and that's completely normal. There's no one in the world can say they aren't afraid of anything and actually be telling the truth. Even Acorn had her fears, but none of them were incredibly pressing at the moment so she was doing just fine.

Poor Theodore Froglen, however, was not doing just fine. Two of his biggest fears were colliding all at once and he was so scared, he could hardly move. Back on the mainland, Froglen lived by a forest pond. It was a very quiet, very peaceful place where nothing too big ever happened. Occasionally in the summers, though, a thunderstorm or two would come rolling over the pond and they always made a tremendous amount of noise and brought rain that pounded against his lilypad house much harder than the usual, calm rain. Lilypad houses are incredibly comfortable and homey, but they don't stand very strong in big storms. So every time one of these storms rumbled around the pond, Froglen would sit in the corner with a blanket wrapped around his head and hope that his house would make it through the nasty weather.

He was also incredibly afraid of heights. His house was a single story (most lilypad houses are) and since he spent almost all his time in the water or hopping through the grass, he had never really gotten a good head for heights. You might think that since he was a frog he would have enjoyed leaping high in the air. The truth is, most frogs fall into two categories. Some frogs do like to see how high they can jump and enjoy this very much. Other frogs like to see how far they can jump and prefer to keep close to the ground and make some distance. Froglen was the second type of frog and felt sick to his stomach anytime he had to stand anywhere higher than a couple stories up. Once he had spent the summer visiting his cousins who were tree frogs, and he had spent the entire vacation in terror of falling out of their treetop dwelling.

So having Acorn ask him to jump as high as he possibly could to catch a rope in the middle of a massive, loud storm was essentially combining both of his worst fears to make one incredibly huge fear. Froglen tried his best to answer Acorn, but what happened instead was that he opened and shut his mouth a few times and his eyes got very wide and frightened. It was not a very promising answer to Acorn's question.

"Mr. Froglen," Acorn said so only the terrified frog could hear her, "I understand that I'm asking something big. Perhaps on another day, we'll have more time to explore any fears that might go with that. Right now, though, there is a very large problem, and I need you to be the one to fix it. So I'm asking you, can you make that jump? Because I believe that you can jump higher than whatever is scaring you and help us all out of this mess and I need you to believe that too. Jump, Mr. Froglen."

Froglen's eyes stopped looking so wide and he looked bravely at his captain. He still couldn't quite find his voice, but he was able to nod and that was more than enough for him and Captain Acorn to understand each other. Squatting low on his shaking legs, he tried to remember everything he had ever learned from other frogs who liked to jump to great heights. He took a deep breath and closed his eyes for a moment. For her part, Acorn was starting to question if he was ever going to move again as the moment stretched on and on. She was just starting to wonder if the newspaper headlines about the sinking of her ship would do her justice (or if they would just be tacky, poorly written stories designed to get more readers) when it finally happened.

With a gigantic leap that later became quite famous in stories about the Golden Acorn, Froglen jumped higher than he ever had before. I genuinely believe that if his cousins from the Amazon had seen him that day they would have been equal parts shocked and proud. Acorn held her breath along with the rest of the crew as Froglen sailed through the air. Froglen focused on his jump and kept his eyes on the rope, even though the rain was stinging his big frog eyes and the thunder was just as loud as ever. All at once, Froglen managed to catch hold of the rope that was flapping wildly in the wind and rain and pull the sail in.

"Well done Froglen!" Captain Acorn cried from the helm of the ship as he slid down the remainder of the rope to land on the deck, and she meant it. She was a very proud squirrel, but she didn't always keep that pride to herself. If someone on the crew did something truly exceptional, Acorn was always the first to give them the praise they deserved. The rest of the crew cheered and whooped and applauded. Even though the storm was still raging on, they had the time to do this now thanks to Froglen. The ship was navigating the frothy, angry seas with a little bit more ease and the wind wasn't nearly as big of a threat. Froglen had truly saved the ship by pulling the rope in.

Froglen looked shocked that he had actually jumped that high, and now that he was safely on the deck, his long, gangly legs were shaking so badly Acorn thought he almost looked like he was dancing. She suddenly felt worried that this poor, brave frog was going to pass out right there in the rain, but he smiled nervously and gave her a very shaky thumbs up. This is not usually the kind of response you should give a captain when they congratulate you on a job well done, but Acorn was more than willing to let it slide given the extraordinary circumstances.

"Froglen!" Acorn yelled through the wind and rain, "I think you had best get something warm to drink and take a breather. Please head below deck."

Froglen nodded appreciatively at his Captain and ran below deck as fast as his nervous, shaking legs would take him.

I can't say that after Froglen's leap that the storm magically vanished. I can't even say that it wasn't a problem anymore. For the rest of that day and part of that night, the crew of the Golden Acorn worked and worked to keep the ship steady through the storm, and when it finally passed Acorn ordered a ship-wide nap for the exhausted crew. I can say, however, that Froglen became a much braver frog that day. He still was, and always stayed, afraid of heights and big storms, but the change was that he didn't see any reason anymore for them to keep him from doing anything. His fears were, after all, just a problem to take care of, and he always felt that he had Captain Acorn to thank for helping him realize that. There's nothing quite like having to face your two biggest fears at the same time to give you a little perspective on them. In fact, years and years later when he was a very old frog, Froglen would often help his grandfrogs face their own fears by telling them about the storm he faced on the sea once and the words the great Captain Acorn had said to him to help him overcome his fear.

CHAPTER FOUR
CAPTAIN ACORN GOES DIVING

There seems to be a point in the life of any great adventurer when they feel the need to discover some great treasure. Acorn hit this stage very suddenly, but this was hardly out of character for her. One day as she pored over the charts in her cabin, the idea came to her.

"Pounce!" she called out loudly, and then she waited. In a moment she heard running footsteps. Before they could slow down to knock on the door, though, there was a loud "oof!" and an even louder "bang!"

"Come in, Pounce," Acorn said calmly. She was very used to Pounce's loud and clumsy entrances at this point.

Pounce opened the door and strolled in, rubbing her nose where she must have slammed it in the door. She tried her best to hide the fact that her nose hurt so bad it was making her eyes water as she walked in and joined Acorn at her table.

"You called, Captain?" she said, still rubbing her nose so that her voice came out nasally and watery.

"Pounce," Acorn said briskly. If she noticed Pounce still rubbing her nose she didn't pay any attention to it. "We've made a lot of voyages together, done a lot of things, but do you know what we're still missing?"

Pounce stopped rubbing her nose and got excited instead. "An espresso machine? Are you finally getting an espresso machine? Because I said it to you last week and I wasn't really sure you heard me when I said it. Even though I said it to you when it was just us and you had asked me how my day was going."

"Pounce, no-"

"But if you did hear me, well, then it's all alright. It really is a smart move if you ask me, captain. I heard some other crew members talking the other day about how long we've been at sea and I think espresso would be just the thing, you know? It would feel like a little bit of home in a cup and then maybe they wouldn't feel so homesick. Of course, I can take care of getting it, you won't even have to worry. At the next port, I'll buy one and set it up for us to use. Oo! I'll even learn how to do that little art stuff on the foam that you like. That way we can-"

"Stop it, Pounce!" Acorn finally yelled, less out of anger and more to be heard over the excited chatter, and brought her paw down hard on the table, something she hated doing. "We're not getting an espresso machine!"

A lesser cat might have sulked or become grumpy after having a request for an espresso machine denied, especially after they had truly started to believe they were getting one and could almost taste the coffee already. Fortunately for Acorn, Pounce was no ordinary cat and, as her name suggested, could easily bounce back from disappointment, which she did now. She nodded a few times to herself as though the denial of the espresso machine was for the best and then asked only a little pointedly.

"So what *else* are we missing?"

Acorn chose to ignore the tone of Pounce's voice and tried to regain the dramatic air she'd had before they wasted precious time on the idea of espresso. "We're missing," she said, slowly building up the drama of the moment, "buried treasure!"

Pounce clapped a paw over her mouth and gave a little gasp of excitement. It was incredibly easy to get Pounce excited. That was one of the primary reasons Acorn enjoyed telling the cat her plans first. It was sort of a test for if the idea was actually a good one, and Pounce's excitement showed that this was a very good idea.

"Yes!" Acorn said dramatically, "If we're going to be anything worth talking about, we need to discover some treasure."

Now Pounce became a little confused, "Why would treasure make us worth talking about? I mean, besides having enough money to buy an espresso machine." It turns out Pounce wasn't as ready to let that go as she might have seemed.

"Pounce, don't you see?" Acorn hardly minded that Pounce was being a little slow to understand because it gave her more time to build up excitement for her plan. "We chart a course to some treasure, and pull it up. After we've split some profit amongst ourselves, to pay the crew a bonus and give us some fantastic souvenirs, we'll distribute the rest to museums and science centers and universities. Think of the learning opportunities, Pounce! All that knowledge to be spread around the world, and I'm the one that's going to bring it to the surface!"

Acorn sighed contentedly. She couldn't quite decide which sounded better: the fame and glory of contributing so greatly to history, or how long her name would last in her own family. She could just picture the schools that would be named after her or the museums with plaques bearing her name. Then she could also see the younger generations of squirrels in her family raising little squirrels of their own long after she was gone, saying things like: "Oh yes, your great-great-great grandmother Acorn, the very famous sea captain, brought that home from her travels. It's our most prized possession. That piece of treasure is our family's legacy. We owe everything to Acorn."

"Ummm. Captain?" Pounce asked timidly, and Acorn suddenly came back to reality.

"Right, well," she said briskly. "Let's be about our business then, Pounce. We have a treasure to find."

It was soon decided that the best place to find their treasure would be just offshore of a well-known chain of islands. The second sister had read a book about pirates once where they had to abandon their treasure as they set sail from an island to escape enemies. When she suggested this to her siblings it seemed like as good a place as any for someone to find a treasure so that is exactly where Acorn decided they should sail the Golden Acorn.

Captain Acorn left Pounce in charge of the crew for the next couple of days to prepare the ship's submarine for a diving expedition while she charted their course. The crew grew more and more excited the longer Acorn stayed in her cabin. Most nights, Pounce joined her to help her look over charts and make their course. More often than not, though, Acorn kept to herself which only fueled the excitement of the crew.

The crew was terribly excited to have located a site for treasure hunting so quickly. As the parents in the front seat listened, it seemed to them that this was far too convenient. But they understood that children's imaginations aren't overly concerned with how convenient something is and more concerned with how exciting it is. It takes an awful lot of work to set up a story and sometimes it's just easier to jump ahead to the exciting parts, which is exactly what the four sisters were doing.

The Golden Acorn weaved in and out of the small islands until, at last, Acorn snapped her compass shut in her paw and called out for Mr. Crockey to lower the anchor. The crew all looked at each other with excited eager faces but said nothing. Acorn was greatly enjoying building the excitement up as she had back in the stadium when she picked her crew, and she stayed still, quietly looking over the side of the deck while the anchor was dropped. After a moment longer of suspense, she turned to face the eager crew on deck, standing in the bright sunshine.

Now, unfortunately, Acorn occasionally suffered from migraines. The sisters had given her this condition after watching their own father suffer from them and understood them to be a sort of a headache that made normal headaches look like a nice, comforting massage by comparison. They weren't entirely sure during Captain Acorn's day what a migraine did or felt like. They only knew that when Daddy got them they needed to be absolutely quiet and that he needed to keep still and be in a dark room. With this knowledge in mind, they gave Acorn the same condition. She didn't get them often, but when she did Pounce was left in charge for a few hours while Acorn lay down in her cabin and moaned things about how terrible it was until she could sleep in the darkness and recover.

So it was incredibly unfortunate that as she turned to face her crew and the sunlight hit her eyes Acorn realized she was getting a migraine. She realized it, but immediately chose to ignore it, which is something people decide to do sometimes when they have a very important thing to do. Acorn believed she had a very important thing to do. If it had been any other kind of adventure, things would have been different. If they were exploring an island that was new to them or racing to beat a world record in sailing, or having a minor battle with an enemy ship, Captain Acorn could have left the whole thing in the very capable hands of her crew. This was different though. This was the stuff of legends. The animal that hauled this treasure to the surface was going to have their name down in history books. She wasn't about to stay on deck and supervise history being made because her head was hurting. Acorn wanted to get her paws dirty.

With that in mind, she tried her best to act as though absolutely nothing was wrong. She shaded her eyes with a single paw and began addressing her crew.

"Animals of the Golden Acorn!" she tried to begin dramatically, but she was squinting her beady little eyes far more than she usually did, so the effect was less than it would have been in ordinary, Acorn circumstances. "I thank you all for your very hard work preparing for this expedition. If we accomplish what we hope to today, the fame of this particular voyage will be far greater than any of my previous ones, and you will all have been a part of it!"

She said this to create enthusiasm for their venture, which is exactly what the crew responded with. They let out a tremendous cheer that was full of smaller whoops and yays all mixed in. Acorn immediately regretted this for her head started pounding and decided it didn't want to stop anytime soon. When the cheering died down, Eli Mousell, the smallest and quietest crew member aboard the Golden Acorn, politely raised his hand and waited.

"What is it Mr. Mousell?" Acorn asked, trying to keep the pounding of her head out of her voice.

"I was wondering, Captain Acorn, ma'am." stammered Mousell very nervously. This was the most he had ever spoken in front of his captain and he was starting to feel his question wasn't worth all the fear and discomfort that came with asking it. "Have you picked who will go with you in the submarine to find the treasure?"

"An excellent question," Acorn said briskly. Mousell immediately felt a lot better about having asked it. "Considering the size of our sub, I will only be able to take one crew member below the surface with me."

The entire crew's shoulders slumped just a little, but they tried to hide their disappointment. All of them knew that if it came down to taking a single animal with her, Captain Acorn would choose Pounce every time.

"Which is just as well." Mousell thought to himself reasonably, "They've known each other the longest. If you're going to be squished in a very tight place with someone for a while, it's probably best to have it be someone you're on a first name basis with."

Still, Acorn announced Pounce as her traveling companion with as much pomp and ceremony as if it was the first time. For her part, Acorn appreciated that Pounce had the good sense to at least act surprised. The reality of the situation was, however, that Pounce hadn't been paying attention to the conversation with the crew at all because she was watching a large colorful fish circling in the water just next to the ship. So when Acorn announced her as her submarine companion, Pounce had been genuinely surprised to hear her name so suddenly. She stood up so straight, and so abruptly that she bonked her head on the underside of the submarine as it dangled above the ship's deck, and had to rub her head the whole time she thanked her Captain for this most prestigious honor.

Soon Captain Acorn and Pounce were safely tucked into the submarine, which the crew had named the Little Acorn, and they were slowly lowered beneath the waves. Pounce, who was incredibly excited to be allowed to spend some time in the submarine was taking full advantage of how exciting the whole adventure was. Mostly her excitement took form in loudly yelling: "Dive! Dive! Dive!"

"Pounce," Acorn groaned softly.

"Dive!" Yelled Pounce, not taking any notice.

"Pounce." Acorn tried again a little louder.

"Dive!" Came the enthusiastic response.

"POUNCE!" Acorn finally bellowed to get the cat's attention.

"Dive?" Pounce answered in confusion, her ears perking up curiously.

"Maybe," Acorn said weakly, "Maybe since this is such a big event, it should be more of a quiet awe sort of thing. You know?"

"Ooooooooooooh." Pounce said softly. "I didn't even think about that. That does seem like the right way to go about this. Right, Captain. Quiet awe. You got it."

Acorn felt rather pleased with herself that she had found a way to quiet things for her poor head without hurting Pounce's feelings in the process. She could be a very brisk squirrel, but she really did care deeply for her first mate and hated the idea of making her sad no matter how badly her head was hurting. She hoped that this would have been the last of things to make her head feel worse, but as with most wishful thinking, she turned out to be very, very wrong.

Now the sisters, who knew very little about how migraines work, had always noticed that their Father's head hurt the most suddenly when they drove up the mountain. Whenever they asked their mother about it she said it had something to do with air pressure and elevation. In the minds of the girls, this translated to mean going up and down great distances when you have a migraine is not the best thing for you. Captain Acorn knew this too, and her smile over the whole adventure was starting to look more and more like a grimace as she and Pounce lowered deeper and deeper into the ocean.

To make matters worse, the Little Acorn was a surprisingly noisy submarine. It made all sorts of chugging and humming and gurgling and whooshing sounds and it made them all the time and all at once. Those noises on their own were bad enough, but they were nothing compared to the steady beeping of the Little Acorn as it searched for the sunken treasure.

"Booooooooooooooop... Booooooooooooooop..... Booooooooooooooop..."

The worst part of it was the pause in between. It was just long enough to make Acorn believe that the beeping had stopped and just short enough to disappoint her by loudly beeping again at top volume. She tried to remind herself that the whole point of all the beeping noises was to find a treasure, so she pushed the Little Acorn to go a little faster. The sooner they had the treasure, she figured, the sooner she would have unimaginable fame and relief from her migraine. Suddenly, the Little Acorn made a series of loud, quick beeps that made Acorn's heart skip a beat itself. There was no treasure immediately in sight, but the submarine was in front of a very large, very dark underwater cave that looked more than a little spooky from the outside.

It was at this point that a small argument started up amongst the sisters. The oldest argued that the treasure wouldn't possibly be there since the pirates had supposedly dropped their treasure in a hurry and the youngest was inclined to agree with her. The two middle sisters felt that that wasn't a particularly important detail and that the cave offered more of a dramatic setting for a treasure to be discovered in. After much back and forth, it was decided that Captain Acorn would at least investigate the cave to be sure, which is what she did, even if there were some grumblings from certain sisters on the subject.

"Pounce," Acorn said when all was finally settled, "I think we ought to investigate that cave. The Little Acorn seems to think we're close, and though I don't like the chances of finding our treasure in there, I think it would be a mistake to pass it by."

"Excellent idea, Captain!" Pounce said agreeably, her voice slowly rising from quiet awe to a normal volume again. While Pounce was a very sweet and caring cat, she usually could only be that if someone outright told her that had something she needed to be sweet and caring about. She wasn't the best at noticing things herself and most of the time it took someone noticing it for her for her to understand. At the moment, she had no idea that Acorn was suffering from a migraine. If she did know, she would have been going to great lengths to take care of her dear captain, but since Acorn hadn't told her anything she was slipping back into her loud, excitable ways. In many ways, Pounce really wasn't all that clever by any means, but she was a loyal friend and a good first mate.

The two animals made their way to the back of the submarine, which wasn't really that far, but took a longer than you might expect because there were a lot of low ceilings and hatch doorways to go through. Pounce repeatedly smacked her head on things and kept rubbing the now very sore spot between her pointed ears. Acorn came much slower following behind. After watching Pounce hit her head the first time, she knew that the last thing she needed when her head was feeling like this was to go around smacking it on thick metal objects. So, being the clever squirrel that she was, she took her time going through each low hanging point of the submarine, taking care to not even brush her ears against the metal.

Pounce set to work preparing the suits while Acorn leaned her head against a metal door frame and felt incredibly thankful that it felt so cool on her fur.

"Right Captain! The suits are all prepped for diving and- are you alright, Captain?"

Acorn was most certainly not alright. Her head was hurting so badly that she could hardly think straight and she was desperately trying not to see double or look directly into the flashing lights of the Little Acorn. She was incredibly concerned with appearing normal, however, and thought that the best way to do that was by smiling. The trouble with trying to look normal when you aren't feeling normal at all is that most of the time you end up looking fairly terrible. Acorn's smile was more of a grimace, and her attempt at an excited face looked more crazed than happy. Pounce looked genuinely horrified for a moment and actually took a step back from her Captain. Acorn immediately changed her face to look more serious and tried to act as if nothing had happened.

The two animals climbed into their suits and secured their helmets. They were very expensive diving suits that Acorn had bought from an outdoor sporting store a few years back. She had probably spent more on them than she should have, but she had liked the weighted belts and that allowed the wearer to walk on the ocean floor and the fancy intercom system that the suits had and so she had spent a little extra. She and pounce hadn't had any use for them at the time but they were certainly coming in handy now.

"Prepared to pressurize the mask on your command, Captain." Pounce said, trying her best to stay formal for the solemn event.

"Proceed," Acorn said regally.

Pounce hit the big red button and their suits began to pressurize. The change in air pressure made Acorn's head throb with pain like never before.

"HOLY WALNUTS!!" Acorn screamed suddenly and so loudly that the microphone made a loud feedback sound and she yelled some more. "Oh great squirrel fur!!"

Pounce's worried face came in close to her mask.

"What is it, Captain?? What's wrong? Are you all right?"

Acorn thought quickly to save the dignity of the moment.

"All fine, Pounce. All fine." she said weakly, "I was just, suddenly overcome with excitement for what today means. Treasure! Yay!" and she held her paws up in the air to reinforce the idea of her excitement.

More than looking unconvinced by Captain Acorn's reason for yelling, Pounce looked genuinely disturbed by her Captain using the word "yay". Sensing that she was in danger of being doubted, Captain Acorn quickly strode past her first mate into the outer chamber of the Little Acorn. Pounce followed behind in confusion but said nothing more about it and sealed the door behind them. Once inside the chamber, Acorn gave an enthusiastic thumbs up to Pounce, who was still looking very confused but hit the release button anyway. The chamber slowly filled with water and in a minute to two animals opened the outer door and they were swimming freely on the ocean floor.

"CAPTAIN ACORN? COME IN CAPTAIN ACORN." Pounce's voice pounded through her ears and the microphone made another screeching sound.

"You're coming in loud and clear." Acorn said, and then added to herself "emphasis on the loud…"

"ROGER THAT CAPTAIN. WE ARE APPROACHING THE CAVE." Pounce bellowed. It seemed that Pounce wasn't really trusting the intercom system in the suits and was making her voice louder as an extra measure to be sure her captain could hear her. The technology was working fine, however, which meant that Pounce was yelling everything in Acorn's ear through a sensitive, high-quality sound system.

"Yes, Pounce. I can see that." Acorn groaned.

"THIS IS VERY EXCITING, CAPTAIN."

"Quiet awe, Pounce. Remember the quiet awe." Acorn pleaded.

"YES OF COURSE CAPTAIN! SORRY!" Pounce replied in a whispery sounding voice that still came through the microphone as shouting. Acorn gave a heavy sigh and would have likely clapped her paw over her face if the suit had allowed.

The two animals carefully entered the cave and turned on their flashlights. Even that sudden light made Acorn's head pound more fiercely than ever and she wondered if she was seeing the flashlight beam or little stars. Pounce continued to whisper at a full volume without ceasing, so Acorn could never get a word in to ask if her first mate was seeing the stars too, or if that was just her.

Round and round the cave they looked, but never saw anything as they went. Just as they were coming what looked like the very back of the cave, poor Captain Acorn began to feel a little wave of disappointment and despair. It was not just that she might never have the legacy that discovering a treasure would bring, but that she felt sick from her head hurting as well. A migraine on its own is a bad enough thing. A migraine and a massive disappointment is another thing altogether. She had just resolved to give up the hunt when her flashlight suddenly glinted on something that made a light flash in her eyes.

"Ugh!" She yelled in pain and gripped her helmet with both paws. After a moment of feeling sick from pain, she careful pointed her flashlight in the same direction, making sure it didn't point directly at whatever had glittered in the cave. It was then that she and Pounce saw several gold coins leading away to a sudden, sharp turn in the cave. She and Pounce quickly swam into the turn, following the glittering trail with their flashlights in the dark until they suddenly came into a huge, inner chamber of the cave.

"Holy Walnuts." Pounce whispered, and this time it was actually a real and quiet whisper.

In the center of the cave was a pile of old sea chests filled and overflowing with gold coins. They spilled all around the cave floor and sparkled in the flashlight beams. All around the gold coins were massive golden plates, chains, and statues. The sisters tried to think of more things that could be made of gold, but they were running out of ideas, so they simply decided that there would be a lot of the few things they could think of instead. The whole pile filled the chamber and stood much taller than the two divers in their suits. Captain Acorn had never seen so much gold in all her life.

The best part of it all was that Pounce had suddenly grasped the full meaning of awed silence. Acorn looked over at her first mate and smiled at the cat's dumbfounded expression and mouth hanging open in wonder. For the first time since they had started their diving adventure, it was absolutely silent. There wasn't any other moment Acorn would have chosen for silence and floated there for several minutes just taking it all in. It was all so glorious she hardly noticed her pounding head anymore.

Acorn and Pounce stayed completely silent as they loaded treasure onto the Little Acorn for the next hour. It seemed that since discovering awed silence, Pounce was now extremely reluctant to break it. When they finally brought in the last gold coin into the submarine, the two animals had to climb over the treasure piled inside just to get back into their seats.

Acorn sat down to start steering the submarine back to the surface but suddenly realized she was seeing stars as her head continued throbbing.

"I think you had better drive, Pounce," she said, unbuckling her seatbelt and moving to switch seats with her first mate.

"Are you sure you're alright, Captain?" Pounce asked happily as she climbed into the driver's seat. She had never been allowed to drive the submarine before so this was the final icing on the cake for making this day perfect. She didn't wait for an answer in her excitement, though, and started driving the submarine so suddenly that Acorn flew backward and landed in the treasure pile where she lay with both paws over her eyes.

It was late afternoon when the Little Acorn resurfaced, and the crew was all waiting silently at the edge of the ship waiting to hear any news as Acorn stumbled back out. As she did so though, she slid on a slippery pile of coins and

a large bunch of treasure slid out with her. She stood in front of her dumb-struck crew for a long moment of silence, before they all erupted into wild cheers and hollers. Acorn waved regally, but weakly as the crew started to chant: "Captain Acorn! Captain Acorn!" as loud as they possibly could. This was one of those rare moments when she truly wished that she hadn't worked so hard to have a revered reputation and that she was just like any other seafaring squirrel.

Even with the crew working as fast as they could, it was night by the time the treasure was fully unloaded onto the ship and they could all admire it. It was then that several crew members nudged Mr. Mousell forward who nervously and quietly (which Acorn appreciated) squeaked: "Please Captain, if we may. We prepared a little surprise for you while you were gone."

Acorn immediately pictured being treated to a spa day or maybe even a quiet orchestra performance to soothe her head. Instead, the crew suddenly revealed a large stockpile of fireworks, all ready to be set off the side of the ship. Acorn realized at that moment that she was largely to blame for the noise that was about to happen.

"If I hadn't tried so hard to be dramatic and get them excited about treasure hunting, they would only be moderately excited and wouldn't even be considering fireworks." She thought bitterly. It wasn't so much that she was actually angry or feeling sorry that she had gotten her crew so excited and more the pain of the migraine talking. Soon enough though, the fireworks were set off and they were the final straw for Acorn's poor pounding head. She covered her ears with both paws and grimaced happily as her crew ooh'ed and aah'ed and cheered some more. She didn't want to take away from the excitement of the crew, but neither did she want to suffer any longer than she had to.

As another firework went off Acorn visibly winced and turned to Pounce. "Pounce," she said. "I have a bit of a headache. I think I'm going to go lie down for a bit."

"No problem, Captain!" Pounce said excitedly, never taking her eyes of the fireworks. "How long will you be in your cabin?"

"Not long at all," Acorn muttered as she left. "No more than a week."

Pounce's ears perked up in curiosity at those words. "A week?" She thought to herself, "She couldn't have meant a whole week…"

But Acorn certainly did. While the fireworks continued late into the night Acorn lay in her cabin with a pillow over her head, moaning. She decided then and there that if it ever was up to her again to decide between sunken treasure and seeing to a migraine, she would see to the migraine every time. Some other animal could get the glory just as long as her head would stop hurting.

CHAPTER FIVE
THE GOLDEN ACORN FINDS A SURPRISE

Since Captain Acorn typically hired an entirely new crew for each of her voyages, there were very few animals, if any besides Pounce, who were familiar with the sort of dangers that might be faced on such a journey. She was known for keeping the details of her upcoming voyage very private. Some animals who sailed with her didn't like this approach. They said it was a strange way to run a ship and that they always felt anxious about what was coming next. Others said that it was a wonderful way to learn and that made them far better sailors than they ever could have hoped it to be.

As for Acorn herself, she had her reasons for conducting her voyages this way. In her mind, letting her crew get surprised by the events of the voyage made for a new generation of competent, seaworthy sailors with every voyage. While she was a very confident squirrel, she was also a mindful one. It was very near and dear to her heart to make sure anyone she took on her crew became the absolute best and could always have a successful career in voyaging. It was part of what made her so beloved as captain. There weren't too animals out there who could boast that they had a recommendation letter from Captain Acorn, and they didn't take that knowledge lightly. Having a letter like that pretty much guaranteed an animal a job anywhere they wanted it.

There was the rare occasion, however, when even Acorn was surprised by something that happened on her voyage. This is, of course, excusable in every way. Acorn couldn't be expected to anticipate every possible adventure, even if she did her best to keep an eye out for dangers. The sea that Acorn loved so much was full of surprises, some wonderful, some dangerous, and some both.

As the Golden Acorn continued sailing after finding the treasure, things seemed to be going very well. The crew was all in high spirits which is to be expected considering that they had just become wealthy. The idea of being rich is often enough to make people very happy, so being actually rich had the crew just giddy. The party and fireworks had lasted all through the night and even when they had run out of fireworks the crew had continued to celebrate, eating snacks and drinking sparkling cider until everyone came crashing down from the sugar rush. So for the next few days, the crew stayed in a sort of happy, carefree daze that made them do their work cheerfully, but not all that diligently.

This, unfortunately, ended up being a problem in certain jobs. Some jobs it didn't really matter if the person doing it was paying all that much attention. No one really minded that the ship's cook, Mr. Turtlestein had been over seasoning things for the last three days as he hummed happily to himself in the ship's galley. No one really cared when the animals in charge of mopping the deck forgot to put out the wet floor signs, causing several unsuspecting animals to slip rather theatrically on the deck. And no one really noticed when the ship's latest laundry had colors and whites mixed together so that several animal's white socks came back as a very festive pink.

It did, however, become a problem when more important jobs weren't done diligently. The worst was when a rather young chipmunk sailor, Timothy Chip, was on lookout duty. Chip was the youngest member of the crew, and had a bit of a problem with being distracted, whether or not there were treasure and fame to daydream about. He was a very nice chipmunk and was an excellent, hard-working crew member, but you had to get him on task and then to stay on task first. Ordinarily, Acorn wouldn't assign jobs like lookout duty to distractible animals, no matter how nice they were, but she was in a bit of a treasure and fame daze herself. So, assigned him to the lookout one afternoon without really thinking about it. Timothy Chip found himself with an incredibly important job that sent him somewhere to sit all by himself with absolutely no one there to make sure he was paying attention to the job he was supposed to be doing.

Chip himself wasn't really much concerned with the fact that he was on lookout duty for the first time and it never crossed his mind that he might not be the best person for the job. Most times if someone is easily distracted, they have absolutely no idea that they are. If they knew, then they could just police themselves and the whole thing wouldn't be a problem. Chip didn't know that he was distractible, and he scrambled up the ropes of the ship until he was perched happily in the lookout.

It was a calm afternoon, with a more gentle wind that pushed the Golden Acorn along at a leisurely pace. Chip took in a huge breath of fresh, sea air that filled his lungs and cheeks (which fill up much, much more than most cheeks) and sighed happily. In a matter of moments, he was happily daydreaming away the day and thinking about what a lucky chipmunk he was to be on such an adventure at such a young age. He leaned forward and rested his chin on his paws, sighing happily. Passing underneath the lookout on her rounds, Captain Acorn noticed that Chip seemed to be a little more relaxed than someone on lookout duty usually should be. Even then, she didn't think anything of it. It was a calm day without a cloud in sight.

As the animals of the Golden Acorn happily went about their work, something in the sea started to churn and move. It was uncomfortably close to the ship, but no one took any notice of it and the Golden Acorn sailed on. The water bubbled and frothed and splashed until something very large and incredibly frightening lifted its head from the waves.

It was a sea serpent from the depths of the ocean.

Or, in this case, a stuffed animal snake that had become jammed between the car seats and the sisters had only just found again. It was massive and had slimy, wet scales that shined green and blue in the sunlight. It flicked its long red tongue out hungrily and watched the Golden Acorn in the distance. To a sea serpent, a ship like the Golden Acorn is a rare and delicious treat, like a chocolate egg with treats inside. Licking his great big serpent lips, he dove down into the water again and started following the Golden Acorn.

When he came alongside the ship, he spotted Timothy Chip high up in the lookout, so he poked his head out of the water and hissed at the little chipmunk. To the sea serpent's surprise, Chip took absolutely no notice of him and kept staring dreamily off into the distance. The sea serpent had never had this happen to him before and sank back beneath the waves to try again. A little ways off from the ship, he lifted his huge tail and brought it back down into the water with a tremendous splash. Timothy Chip only sighed happily and blinked slowly in his dreamy daze. The sea serpent couldn't believe the terrible luck he was having and dove down one more time. It wasn't until the sea serpent was looking at the Golden Acorn straight on and sitting directly in its path that someone (though not Chip) noticed him. Pounce let out a strange yell that was somewhere between a battle cry and a scream of terror, and all the animals on deck turned to see what she was carrying on about.

The effect of seeing a huge sea serpent bearing over the ship was instantaneous. As all the animals started rushing about like ants, looking for weapons and their Captain, the sea serpent grinned a hideously huge grin. I think he was starting to feel a little offended that no one had taken notice of him and wanted to be seen and admired before he started attacking. Now the crew had seen him and was in a panic to defend themselves, so all felt right again and the horrible monster could continue his attack on the ship. He was angrier than he might have been if he had been noticed right away, which only drove home that Chip had made a terrible mistake in not alerting the crew sooner. A sea serpent is hard enough to fight, let alone one that feels he's been insulted by his target.

The sea serpent watched the crew scramble around the deck for a moment longer before he started snapping and tearing at the sails, almost as if they were the wrapping on his tasty treat. The crew of the Golden Acorn was still running around in a panic while this happened. Some animals like Pounce were quickly arming themselves and preparing to fight. Others were running around with weapons screaming in terror, which is a very stupid thing to do because they were much more likely to hurt themselves or a crew member than the actual dangerous sea serpent itself. Some crew members were simply staring up at the beast in dumbfounded horror and not moving a muscle.

For his part in the lookout, Chip was becoming startlingly aware of exactly what was happening and the horrible reality that it was almost entirely his fault. There wasn't much time, however, for him to feel sorry for himself. The serpent was still tearing at the sails and the lookout was the most dangerous place to be at the moment. The Golden Acorn was shaking and trembling under the stress of the attack and it was all Chip could do just to hold on and not be thrown from his perch. He was shaking almost as much as the ship and holding on to the railing with both paws, but it seemed like he was doomed.

Suddenly, a shrill battle cry sounded from below. Unlike Pounce's shout, this battle cry didn't have a trace of fear in it and it was loud enough and powerful enough (although a little squeaky) to make the sea serpent pause and look around curiously. On the deck below, Captain Acorn stood with a sword in one hand and her pistol in the other. She yelled unintelligibly up at the sea monster which did less to scare him and more to confuse him. Still, it did what she had hoped for: it gave Chip the opportunity to grab a nearby rope and slide down to the deck, which was not necessarily safe but was a great deal safer than dodging teeth from a very small perch in the sails.

He landed with a thud right at the feet of his captain. Acorn was very aware of Chip's presence, but never broke her eye contact with the beast and continued to glare furiously at him.

"Mr. Chip." Acorn said frostily, "Would you be able to explain why my beloved ship is being snacked on by a sea monster?"

Chip was not able to explain it and only stared up at the beast in mute terror. Realizing that scolding the terrified chipmunk was more of an after battle sort of activity, Acorn stepped out in front of Chip and brandished her sword. The sea serpent looked at Acorn curiously, seemingly wondering how something the size of one of his teeth could possibly stand up to him. But the sea monster wasn't accounting for the fact that while Acorn may have only been the size of one of his teeth, she had courage the size of his whole slimy, scaly body. Deciding that this little squirrel was a great place to start the main course, the serpent suddenly launched himself towards the ship's deck and Acorn. But Acorn rolled nimbly out of the way and the monster stubbed his nose quite badly against the wooden deck.

There was a horrible moment for the crew, who couldn't see their captain past the creature's head, where they thought that he had smashed her to bits. A moment later, though, Captain Acorn sprang onto the railing and called out:

"To me, animals of the Golden Acorn! To me! Dodge it! Don't let it strike!"

The other animals finally stopped running around in a panic and started running around with purpose, which looks almost the same but does a lot more good. The sea serpent kept striking at different points on the ship but missed every time as all the animals kept scattering and dodging his huge jaws.

This plan was very good for not letting any crew members be eaten by the sea monster at the moment, but the Golden Acorn was slowly starting to show the strain of having a massive creature repeatedly headbutt it, and the sea serpent himself was starting to get frustrated with his lack of results. Acorn was desperately trying to think of a plan that would save not only her crew but her beloved ship as well. However, it's incredibly difficult to think of a plan when the majority of your attention is going to dodging a sea monster that's trying to eat you. As it was, the sea serpent came up with a new plan first. If he couldn't get past the ship to the goodies onboard, then he would eat its snack with the wrapper still on it.

It stopped trying to pounce on the crew members individually. Instead, it slithered its great big head back into the sea. For a moment, the crew thought that the attack was over and they all started to cheer in relief, but Acorn knew better. She watched the surface of the water carefully.

"Hush!" She yelled to her crew, but they kept cheering. "Quiet! All of you!"

The animals all fell silent and looked at her in confusion. Acorn sniffed the air, wrinkling up her nose and waiting.

"Captain," Pounce whispered, "I think it's gone."

At that moment, the sea serpent burst out of the water again. This time, though, he opened his hideous jaws wide and started to bite the front of the ship. He didn't just bite it though, he was slowly gnawing on it, and with each move, the Golden Acorn was pulled a little deeper into its mouth. The monster intended to eat the ship whole. Panic started again on the ship. Even Acorn was briefly shocked and covered her mouth with one paw in horror. She wasn't shocked for long though. She loved nothing in the world so much as her beloved Golden Acorn, and seeing it slowly munched on by a sea serpent filled her with a unique kind of rage that was far larger than herself.

She launched herself forward towards the beast. She had long since dropped her pistol and sword when she was dodging the teeth, but that didn't stop her from slapping the creature on the nose and pushing against it with all her might. Not knowing what else to do, the rest of the crew rushed forward and copied Acorn. I think they all thought that it was all part of some brilliant plan she had, but the reality was that Acorn was so furious she would have jumped into the monster's belly if she thought that would have taught it a lesson. So basically, nothing was really happening except the serpent kept getting more of the ship into its mouth bit by bit. It very much seemed like the Golden Acorn was going to be swallowed whole.

In the end, Timothy Chip had the idea that saved the Golden Acorn. The third sister had once read that in a shark attack, the best thing you can do is punch the shark in the gills or eyes. To her, it seemed like an appropriate fact to insert in the story, and so she did. Chip suddenly had an idea about what he could do. Since he was so small, it was easy for him to dash in between the fighting animals and get up alongside the sea monster's head and look around. He was hoping that he could hit him in the gills because the eyes on the monster made him feel sort of sick, but when he couldn't find them he knew what he had to do, no matter how unpleasant it was going to be. Climbing up onto the railing closest to one of the serpent's eyes, Chip took a deep breath, squeezed his paw into a tight fist, and hit the sea serpent in the eye with all his might.

He was so small, and the eye was so big (it was actually larger than Chip himself), that at first, he thought he hadn't done anything at all. All that happened was the eye stopped looking straight ahead and locked on the frightened chipmunk instead. This was a rather horrible thing to see and it scared Chip so much that he almost gave up trying to help right then and there. Still, all of Acorn's speeches about bravery and living life to the fullest came flooding to him at that moment, and he wanted more than anything to make his captain proud, even if that meant hitting the nasty, slimy eyeball again. This time, he took both paws and started smacking and hitting the eyeball as though it were a punching bag, and this time he got a more promising reaction. The sea serpent made a strange groaning noise that made the rest of the crew look around in surprise, but the best part was that the creature moved back just a little. Acorn looked around wildly for what had made the sea serpent move and saw Chip beating away at the eyeball – and looking absolutely sick to his stomach.

"Well done, Chip!" She cried enthusiastically, "Keep it up! Everyone! Do what Chip is doing! Attack the eyes!"

The sea serpent suddenly found itself being poked, kicked, and punched in the eyes, which is incredibly painful even if it's being done by some very small paws and feet and you are a huge sea monster. After several minutes of this, with the animals of Acorn's crew beating at the serpent and the serpent slowly inching back, it gave up. All at once, it let go of the Golden Acorn entirely and slipped back into the water.

This time, the crew all stayed quiet and watched their captain as she sniffed the air once again and looked for any signs of the great beast.

"Look!" Froglen suddenly yelled, and everyone turned to see what he was pointing at. Far off in the distance, the animals could just see the sea serpent. He was scooting away in the water clumsily and at an alarming pace, eager to put all possible distance between himself and the Golden Acorn.

At last, all the animals felt they could erupt into cheers of victory and Acorn smiled proudly at her ship. True, there was certainly some damage done and a lot of repair work was going to be needed, but the important thing was that her ship was still her ship, in one piece and sailing proudly. Turning around she scanned the faces of her crew.

"Where is Mr. Chip?" she called out sternly.

All the animals fell silent and moved as far away from Chip as they could without being obvious. So Chip was left standing alone and shaking like a leaf in front of his captain. Acorn walked straight up to him with a stern frown and looked him up and down while he continued to shake uncontrollably.

"I don't think," Captain Acorn began quietly, "That I need to tell you how serious it is to slack off on lookout duty."

Chip shook his head and his shoulders and tail drooped depressingly low. But Acorn smiled suddenly at him. She certainly felt irritated that her ship had almost been eaten whole, but more than irritated, she felt incredibly proud to have a crew member who had responded so well under pressure, and she wanted him to know it.

"Mr. Chip," she went on while he looked at her in confusion for smiling, "You did a very brave and smart thing. The Golden Acorn and all of us on her would be in the belly of a sea serpent right now if it wasn't for you. I am, and will always be incredibly grateful."

And while she reached out and warmly shook his paw, the whole crew cheered wildly again and clapped enthusiastically for their youngest crew member.

"Captain Acorn, ma'am." Chip stuttered nervously, not used to getting so much one on one attention from such a great squirrel. "May I ask for something?"

"What would that be?"

"Can I not- That is, I would very much like to never be on lookout duty ever again."

Acorn smiled bigger than she ever had at her young crew member and the nervous chipmunk relaxed a little.

"Mr. Chip, I think that is an excellent idea."

CHAPTER SIX
CAPTAIN ACORN IS DIPLOMATIC

O ccasionally in her voyages, Captain Acorn would make some sort of side stop at the request of someone else. Normally, she didn't like having any destination set for her and preferred to go where the sea took her, but these occasions were rarely a simple errand that she was running for a friend. Twice now she had been the very squirrel who delivered peace negotiations between warring islands, and once she even brought back a sample of plant life to the Squirrel Observatory for Science and Discovery, but they had only put a plaque on a park bench in her honor so she had decided not to work with them again.

On this particular voyage, Acorn had one such stop scheduled. The otters of the Southern Otter Clans on Acorn's mainland home had asked Acorn to establish contact with the northern dwelling Penguins in the hopes that they could start up an ice trade. If it was successful, it would totally revolutionize the otter economy while bringing the penguins a sort of prestige they had never had before. Mainland animals had only in the last year or so established contact with the penguins and both sides wanted to keep that connection strong. For her part, Acorn wanted to have her name stamped on that success story. So in the midst of all her voyaging, the Golden Acorn was scheduled for a very particular stop at the Northern Penguin's Island.

Like the Bunny Islanders, the Northern Penguins were not to be taken too lightly. It's not that they were particularly war-minded penguins, and it wasn't that they were fancy like the rabbits. The main thing about the Northern Penguins was that they liked things done in a very particular way and once they found what that way ought to be, they never did it differently again. This led to them developing an incredibly complex set of rules and etiquette that was unlike anything any mainland animals had ever seen before.

While it may have seemed like the Bunny Islanders were like this too, there was one glaring difference. The Bunny Islanders had one rule: be fancy. The Northern Penguins had roughly one hundred and fifty rules on the proper way to be fancy, and that wasn't something they were even overly concerned with. There were rumors on the mainland that some poor animal was still counting up all the studied and recorded rules the Northern Penguins had for how to properly present a fish to your younger cousin on his thirteenth birthday.

Captain Acorn was a well educated and very smart squirrel. She was the type of animal who knew all the best ways to say hello and goodbye, and always knew exactly which piece of silverware to use at a dinner party and when (which is something very few people still know how to do and most are actually just pretending they know). Still, for all of Acorn's knowledge, she only knew general etiquette that was acceptable on the mainland and largely in use in neighboring island communities like the Bunny Islanders. Northern Penguin etiquette was almost completely unknown to her. She had been incredibly disappointed when she had gone to her local library before the voyage to get a book on penguin etiquette only to find that only one had ever been written.

She was even more disappointed to read it and find that it gave a very incomplete picture of the subject. We have to give her a little grace here because she wasn't fully comprehending how little was actually known about the Northern Penguins. In the end, she had visited the Squirrel Observatory for Science and Discovery (and she did so turning up her nose at the park bench with her name on it) and asked them to make her a booklet of their notes on the penguins and their ways. Between the library book and the small guidebook that the squirrels at the observatory had put together for her, Captain Acorn felt a little more confident about the meeting as they drew closer to the Northern Penguin's lands, but not as confident as she would have liked to be.

"Land ho!" Cried Froglen from the lookout, and all the animals rushed to the side of the ship to catch a glimpse as it came into full view.

The Northern Penguins lived on a large, frigid island with wide pebble beaches and snowy inland hills. As the Golden Acorn glided into the bay, the crew could see young penguins sifting thoughtfully through pebbles on the beach and older penguins going to and fro between the large domed houses of the penguin town. The Northern penguins didn't like living in large cities and instead preferred to form quaint villages where everyone knew everyone else. Everything about the island-dwelling coming into view seemed idyllic but equally solemn and serious.

Soon the Golden Acorn had dropped anchor and a selected number of the crew climbed into the rowboat to go ashore. Acorn couldn't take as many crew members ashore with her as she would have liked. This was largely because, coming from the mainland, the animals of the Golden Acorn weren't all that used to cold weather in the north and were bundled up so completely that each crew member took the space of two in the little rowboat.

As the last selected crew member, a stork named McFeathers, dropped into the rowboat with a muffled "oof" from being bundled all the way up to his beak, Acorn shook her head in dismay.

"You'll all be in a load of trouble if we capsize on the way to shore" she muttered. She was a little more irritable than usual, but that was largely from feeling nervous about meeting the penguins and being very cold herself. She did have a large parka on and a scarf and mittens that her mother had knitted for her, but it still didn't quite feel like enough so she kept wrapping her large, bushy tail around her body for extra warmth.

She probably would have been warmer if she had sat down in the boat amongst her crew but she was standing in the front of the boat instead, looking out over the frigid waves. The youngest sister had recently seen a painting of George Washington crossing the Delaware River while standing heroically in the bow of the boat and she thought his stance was the perfect attitude for a famous squirrel like Acorn. So Acorn stood tall and proud with the freezing wind tossing her whiskers and turning them to icicles.

As they drew nearer to the pebbled beach, the young penguins on the shore began to take notice of them and started waving towards the town. By the time Captain Acorn and her crew started clambering out of the boat and onto the beach, a large crowd of penguins was coming towards them. They were just far enough away that Acorn still had time to turn to her crew and whisper urgently:

"Now remember. These penguins are very particular, so everyone better have their best manners on and do exactly as I do."

For most of the crew, this wasn't a problem at all and they all gave quiet signs of understanding like thumbs up or conspiratorial winks. Only a few crew members looked like they weren't really ready to make good on that expectation. Among them was Crockey who was looking absolutely sullen and miserable. To be fair to him, it was very cold, and being a cold-blooded animal in this weather felt like murder to him. Even when you are cold, though, you should always try your best to keep a good attitude because it's not the fault of those around you. They have absolutely no control over the temperature the same as you.

Captain Acorn turned back towards the penguins who had now reached them and the two groups stood awkwardly for a moment, staring at each other. Then a very important looking penguin stepped forward from his group and looked intensely at the Golden Acorn crew. It was difficult to say exactly what made him look important. Most of the crew thought it was because he was taller than the rest and McFeathers thought it was because his feathers looked smoother and shinier than any of the other penguins. Acorn, however, thought it was because of the way he held himself, with his head looking straight on and his beak intent on the visitors. In a lot of ways, Acorn was the closest to the truth. Penguins, being very dignified creatures, will try to look like they are important at all times and only the ones who actually have some responsibility achieve the look without trying too hard.

Not wanting to be outdone, but feeling a little nervous herself, Acorn stepped out from the group and mirrored the important penguin's stance. She didn't have a beak to stare down and settled instead for looking regally past her frozen, scrunched up nose. The important penguin took another step forward and said in a deep squawking voice:

"Greetings, travelers. Welcome to Ice Harbor Island, the capital island of the Northern Penguins. May you always have a pebble in your home and feathers near your heart."

He then looked expectantly at Acorn. She gave a sudden start, remembering that there was a very specific response that she was supposed to give in this situation to be polite. Acorn fumbled for a moment in her jacket pocket to get out her little booklet before remembering that she had spent the last week memorizing the response and already knew it by heart.

"And may you always have someone to huddle with against the cold." Acorn returned. She said it confidently enough but still looked around at the surrounding penguins for approval. For their part, the crew was simply impressed that Acorn was doing so well in the situation. Mr. Mousell thought that it was rather admirable how confident their captain was, even though Acorn was feeling less confident than she ever had before, which just goes to show how far you can get in life by acting confident even if you don't feel it.

Even then there was a long pause in the proceedings, and the crew of the Golden Acorn awkwardly waited for something to happen. The Northern Penguins, it seemed, were a quiet group of birds, or at least they were very quiet towards visitors and didn't have a whole lot to say to animals who weren't attuned to their ways. Still, the penguin who seemed to be in charge of things at the moment nodded solemnly and deeply towards Acorn and her party and gave a wide sweeping gesture with his flipper that seemed to mean they should follow him.

This turned out to be incredibly difficult to do, at least respectfully. Not long before this adventure that took place during this particular car ride, the four sisters had watched a documentary with their father about penguins and the main thing they took away from the experience was the hilarious way that penguins walked, shuffling forward bit by bit and bobbing up and down in the process. The Northern Penguins walked this same way. They shuffled back towards the penguin village with the crew of the Golden Acorn following behind. The obvious side effect of walking like this, however, is that it's incredibly slow going and you never get anywhere all that quickly. For animals like Acorn and Pounce who were used to moving with a certain level of speed and agility, this slow, shuffling and bobbing walk was painfully awkward. Ultimately, they ended up taking a step, waiting about five seconds for some space to open up behind the shuffling penguins, and then taking another step that closed up the gap all over again.

In the end, it took about thirty minutes for them to go what would have taken Acorn about ten minutes to walk. The majority of the crew spent this time feeling somewhere between awkward and grumbly. Acorn, however, was frantically consulting her little guidebook and trying to refresh her mind on all matters penguins for the thousandth time. Eventually, the whole crowd stopped in front of one of the largest buildings in the small town, and the penguin leader made the same sweeping gesture with his flipper again.

"Please come inside." He said warmly. He also gave a little smile which did a great deal to help Acorn and her crew relax a little in their new surroundings. "You all must be very cold and want to warm up."

This may seem like an odd thing to say since he could very obviously see that all the animals from the Golden Acorn were bundled up head to toe. He said this not because he was a dumb penguin who couldn't see the obvious, but because he was trying to be kind and validate how cold they felt. More often than not, someone who is used to the cold telling you that it's cold out will make you feel loads better for feeling chilly yourself.

As it was, not a single animal from the crew took his statement as an insult and they all crowded around the door to be the first one to get out of the cold. Ordinarily, Acorn would have been the first through the door since it was her right as captain to be first in anything she wanted. But on this particular occasion, she let her crew struggle and strain against each other to get through the door while she stood back and watched. She had hoped to look like the cold wasn't really bothering her, but this proved to be a mistake. The wind was picking up and it seemed to be incredibly good at finding any part of her that wasn't bundled up and immediately freezing it. This meant that her tail and cheeks were constantly getting slapped by the wind. But worse than either of those was the little gap between her scarf and hat that kept letting the wind bite at the back of her neck. Even with her lovely chestnut fur, she felt every bit of that icy, biting wind. By the time she was able to get through the door herself, her teeth were chattering and she couldn't feel her face.

This, however, was a moment when Captain Acorn's greatness shone through. Even though the penguins around her, unfazed by the cold, were worriedly ushering her inside, she kept smiling and nodding politely at their concern and telling them through stiff, frozen cheeks that she was all right, even though she didn't feel like she was at all. If Acorn didn't like something people were bound to hear about it, but neither was she a complainer. She would have probably gotten a lot of sympathy for complaining if she had, but she was intensely aware that she was a guest and didn't want to offend anyone in the slightest, so she kept smiling much warmer than she felt and eventually the penguins stopped worrying. It was a tremendous moment of grace on her part. It would have been a thousand times easier for her to complain and make sure everyone knew she was miserable and cold, but she chose to do the hard thing and stay polite and friendly.

Someone was complaining, however, and a little too loudly for the situation. Crockey had been one of the first animals through the door, but by the way he was talking, you would have thought the penguins had left him outside for a couple hours before they let him in.

"Why is it so cold here?" He hissed to any of his crew members close enough to listen to him, whether they wanted to or not. "You think they would have turned up the heat before we got here. I'm freezing to death! Look at my nose, Chip! It's frozen! My nose was never meant to be frozen. These penguins sure don't look out for their fellow animal..."

To make matters worse, the meeting hall they had been ushered into was a large room that was more than a little echoey. So even though Crockey had intended to complain just to his closest neighbors, he essentially ended up complaining to the whole room. Even a few penguins had turned to see who was talking.

To be fair, Jacob Crockey didn't have fur or feathers like a lot of other crew members, so he was significantly colder than most. Still, Froglen was in the same situation as him and he wasn't saying anything rude or whiny, so it seems that Crockey was just being that difficult.

Fortunately for the situation, and before it could get any worse, McFeathers smacked Crockey upside the head with his large wing with a loud "Shhh!". He actually meant the shush to be quiet, but in the wide open hall, his voice carried much farther than he had been anticipating and it echoed enough that a few more penguins looked back towards them in curiosity. Still, Crockey got the message and fell silent, even if it was an extremely grumpy silence.

Acorn made a mental note to quietly thank McFeathers later, but at the moment the penguin leader had strolled to the far side of the room that looked much more important than the side of the room near the door. The other penguins had stopped and were forming a little half circle that left a wide open space on the floor. The penguin leader was taking a seat in a massive chair made of ice across the open space and was motioning politely for Acorn to take a seat in another one of the chairs that were near him. Above the head penguin's chair, a flag was pinned on the wall. It was half white and half black in a diagonal, and in opposite corners, there was a black penguin silhouette on the white side and a white penguin silhouette on the black side. Acorn remembered from her guide book that this was the Northern Penguin national flag, and from the way the other penguins looked at the room and the flag they seemed to be in a very important political room. The whole set up looked rather like a courtroom, but one that's made of ice and full of penguins.

Cautiously stepping forward, Acorn took a seat on the chair offered to her and tried not to wince at how cold it made her tail feel. The penguins were all looking at her expectantly, and she had a sudden, scared feeling that she was supposed to speak first. She hurriedly flipped through the pages of her little booklet until she came across a little-underlined paragraph:

"When meeting with penguins for a political matter. It is actually customary for the visitor to start the talks. They are expected to do so by first singing a verse from a song that best describes them as an animal. Immediately following this, the visitor is expected to state their business in visiting the penguins. While this may seem unnatural to a foreigner. Northern Penguins believe this is the best way to learn more about a visitor quickly and helps them evaluate if that animal can be trusted."

Acorn far preferred having people sing about her instead of having to do the singing herself, but she was very aware that her international reputation was being decided by the penguins here, and she didn't want to let herself or her crew down. So she carefully stood up, cleared her throat a little, and started to sing. It was a song that she had heard in college that had first made her want to go to sea and it always gave her a little extra boost of confidence.

The penguins were all nodding appreciatively as she sang, but the crew of the Golden Acorn was more than a little confused. They didn't have the advantage of Acorn's little booklet, and none of them had bothered to do any research

about the Northern Penguins on their own before they came. So from their perspective, their beloved Captain had seemingly lost her mind and was humiliating herself. You can imagine how relieved they were when the song was over and the Penguins all cheered and clapped politely and they realized that it had all been on purpose. Most of the crew felt their respect grow for their captain and her ability to handle almost any social situation. The only one who didn't seem impressed was Crockey, who snorted rudely and made an unkind comment about "strange traditions". If Acorn heard him, she didn't acknowledge it. She was more relieved than anyone to have the song over and more than willing to discuss business with the penguins, which was more of her strength.

"Esteemed penguins of the North," she began, taking a seat again and doing a better job this time of concealing how cold it made her tail. "I come as an ambassador from the Otter Clans with a trade proposition."

The head penguin nodded as though he already knew about the proposal. Penguins can be a little self-important, and if they can look and act like they know something without trying too hard, they will. Acorn paused as the head penguin nodded, but when he said nothing she continued cautiously.

"The Otters believe that your most excellent ice would greatly help them in their fishing industry and that they would then be able to ship fish as far as your islands. They would, of course, agree to withhold any cost of the fish as a repayment for the ice. I have with me a folder outlining the proposal and all of its finer points."

At this, the crew members all fidgeted uncomfortably. None of them had realized exactly what they had been signing up for when they volunteered to go ashore, so they were a little nervous when Acorn pulled out a folder as thick as a brick. Combing through the finer points of a trade agreement seemed to them to be just about as exciting as watching ice melt. If I'm being honest, it's not much more exciting to write about. Fortunately for the crew, the oldest sister had been the one who knew the most details about business and trade deals, and she had just run out of things to say. So the head penguin simply nodded again, but this time he also rose to his feet and addressed the whole crowd.

"The guests have a business proposal," he reported like none of the animals could hear what he and Acorn had been talking about. In actuality, there was an old penguin social rule that said business dealings must always be declared twice, first to the person you were doing business with and then to a witness. Penguins seemed to think that this kept more animals honest. "This calls for the first toast!"

The surrounding penguins all cheered happily and started chatting amongst themselves as server penguins came from a side door and started passing out steaming glasses. Acorn took advantage of the happy chatter and general distractedness to frantically flip through her booklet for clues. On a page about business procedures filled with her own notes and reminders, she found a little side passage that said:

"Since business affairs are such a rare occurrence amongst penguins, it is most often treated as a special occasion. That means penguins will involve toasting with a beverage of their choice. Toasts may include their visitors health, safe travels, and themselves."

She snapped the booklet shut as a penguin offered her a steaming cup and remembered to say "Thank you for the warmth.", which was the customary thank you when offered a drink by a penguin.

Now the glasses that the penguin servers passed around were filled with a drink very unique to the Northern Penguins. It was a spiced fish cocoa. Penguins love this drink, but if you don't like fish, and you do like cocoa, you would definitely find this beverage almost impossible to drink without making a face. Acorn could smell it as they walked up to her with it, but she managed to keep her face smiling and polite.

Her crew was a little more nervous about the drink and were all struggling a little more to hide their feelings on it. Several animals had to pretend that they had a cough as they choked on the smell, and Pounce even had to cover her nose with a scarf and tell the penguin closest to her that her nose was still feeling a little frozen. Crockey, however, openly made a disgusted face when a penguin handed him a glass and the penguin looked at him in confusion. From across the room, Acorn cleared her throat loudly enough that Crockey looked in her direction. She gave him an intense stare that absolutely said, *You will drink this spiced fish cocoa and you will be polite about it!* He grew a little more sullen, but took the glass all the same. Now the moment had come. The head penguin rose to his feet and lifted his glass high.

"To the crew of the Golden Acorn," he said, "May your ship always sail with the speed of a thousand penguins!" And he took a long sip along with all the other penguins.

After a moment longer of hesitation, the crew of the Golden Acorn raised their glasses as well and took a sip. It seemed that suddenly several crew members' colds got much more intense because there was a great deal more coughing in the room. Pounce even made a strangled sneezing noise that brought spiced fish cocoa squirting out her nose. For her part, Acorn felt like she had never tasted anything more disgusting in all her life. The fish taste and the cocoa taste didn't not at all go well together. To her it tasted like a fish who had never taken a bath in its life had rubbed itself in chocolate and called it perfume. She had to scrunch her nose up higher than she ever had before just to get herself to swallow. When she did though, she tried to smile widely around the fish taste and let out a fake, but content "Mmmmm!"

The crew all followed suite and started making yummy noises of their own and complimenting the penguins nearest to them.

"Delicious!"

"Amazing!"

"How... Fishy!"

"And Chocolatey!"

"I would love to have this recipe!"

Only one crew member didn't make any effort to hide his disgust with the cocoa. Crockey made a loud retching noise (probably louder than he actually felt about the cocoa) and then did a thing that made Acorn angrier than anything had on this voyage yet: He complained, and loudly.

"UGH!" he croaked and several penguins looked at him in alarm. "It's disgusting! I don't like it at all! Why would anyone think this is good?"

Several penguins gasped and one particularly upset penguin walked up to Crockey and snatched the little mug back with a very offended "Hmph!" Any penguins who weren't watching Crockey's rudeness were looking intently at Captain Acorn, including the head penguin. This was the most unexpected thing to happen in several years of penguin history and, even though they were feeling incredibly insulted by Crockey's actions, they were very curious to see if Acorn could salvage the etiquette of the situation. Northern Penguins only have around three different rules for dealing with a rude outburst because they were so few and far between as long as everyone was following the rules.

Forgetting her booklet completely, Acorn leaped to her feet and immediately turned to the head penguin. "Would you please excuse me?"

The penguin leader nodded graciously and Acorn hurried towards the door, but not before she had hissed "Outside. Now." at Crockey. Pounce let out a little "ooo" that was not at all helpful in the situation.

Crunch, crunch, crunch. Captain Acorn stomped outside into the snow with Crockey in tow. When she had gone a little way down the path towards the ship, she turned to face the grumpy crocodile. She was a little embarrassed to see that all the other animals, crew members and penguins alike, were all crowding around windows back at the meeting hall to watch what she would do. But like I said, nothing this far outside of the rules had happened to the penguins in a long time and the crew was getting sort of swept up with all the excitement.

For his part, Crockey had an expression on his face that only made Captain Acorn more frustrated. It's the face that someone makes when they've been behaving horribly, but don't think that they've done anything wrong. So they act like they're being unjustly treated by being singled out for punishment. Acorn scrunched her nose tighter than she ever had before out of sheer anger.

"Crockey." She started coldly, and not just because it was windy and snowy outside. "Do you know what ranking I have amongst captains in Seaside Monthly Magazine?"

"Number one?" Crockey guessed sullenly and in a voice that said he wasn't sorry for his actions at all.

"Number one." Captain Acorn nodded. She started pacing in front of the disgraced crocodile with her hands clasped behind her back, which was no small feat considering how poofy her jacket was. Still, she knew it made her look more regal and authoritative so with a bit of stretching she found a way to manage it. "And do you know how I came to hold that title?"

"By being the best?" Crockey guessed again, even more sullenly.

"By being the best!" Acorn said, so angrily her voice squeaked in a very undignified way. "The best Crockey! I have an international reputation. That might not mean anything to you since *you* don't have one, but to animals who do, it is a very big deal. I didn't work to get where I am now just to have some ungrateful crocodile embarrass me in front of one of the most distinguished group of birds my crew has ever met! Do I make myself clear?"

Crockey muttered something that sounded like a yes in his most sullen voice yet.

"Honestly, Crockey." She sighed in exasperation, and pinched the bridge of her scrunched up nose. "Do you even want to be on this voyage? Because you are most certainly not acting like it."

Crockey only looked down at his leathery feet. He wasn't looking down because he felt embarrassed by his actions like someone might when they realize they've been doing something rude. His looking down was the grumpy and angry kind, where you can't glare at the person scolding you but you still want to glare at something so your feet get the worst of your angry stare.

Acorn knew what he was doing but she genuinely didn't care anymore, and she stomped past her sullen crew member to return to the penguin leader. She was muttering very angrily under her breath as she went and her whiskers were twitching furiously as she stomped, which only made more icicles form on them. She was also glaring at her feet as she went, which is probably why she didn't see the penguin leader until she had bumped right into his great, feathery belly with her furry head.

They both looked at each other in surprise. Acorn looked surprised because she had had no idea that he was there and she didn't know what to say in this situation because she had left her booklet inside. The penguin leader looked surprised because he had just spent the last thirty seconds thinking that at any moment Captain Acorn would notice him standing there and look up and he had only been head-butted for his troubles.

Captain Acorn was still furious at Crockey, but now she was incredibly embarrassed as well, which had a very rare effect on her. She was at a complete loss for words and simply stood with her small squirrel mouth hanging open with icicles forming fast on her whiskers. Fortunately for her, the head penguin seemed to finally have more to say than simply nodding or making a toast.

"I know," said the head penguin solemnly, "that we have a reputation for having a lot of rules and traditions and that many animals from your home have been studying them. But has anyone from your home studied *why* we have all of our rules and traditions?"

Acorn shook her head silently and an icicle fell from her whiskers.

"We have them," the penguin leader continued, kindly choosing to ignore the whisker icicle and look out to the bay instead, "because we respect each other. We penguins want to show each other how important we all are to one another and so we have rules that keep us on track. But do you know what the most important penguin rule is?"

Again Captain Acorn shook her head, and again an icicle fell from her whiskers.

"It is to try." the penguin finished with a smile, "Because if you try, almost all of the other rules are quick to follow. Trying to show someone respect, is the best way to start showing them respect."

He waddled his feet around to face Captain Acorn, and Acorn waited patiently while he turned. He sighed happily and smoothed the feathers of his chest with his wings. "You have been trying very hard today, Captain Acorn. If any animal in the trade proposal you bring will try as hard as you to show respect, then I believe we absolutely can be in business."

He held out a wing and Acorn shook it happily, remembering to only shake it twice before letting go because this was a business handshake and not a friendly handshake, which called for three shakes.

"Shall we go back inside?" The head penguin asked.

"Let's," said Acorn curtly, but much warmer than the chilly air around them. "We still have a lot of business to discuss."

"Ah yes," The head penguin nodded wisely, "I'm sure it will take some time. I'll order more spiced fish cocoa so we have enough to last."

"Oh!" Acorn said tactfully, "More cocoa?"

"Of course!" The head penguin said cheerfully, "penguin tradition calls for at least six cocoa toasts while conducting a business affair. You can leave your crew mate out here if you like. He was the only one who didn't like it so that will solve that problem." Fortunately, he was already waddling back towards the meeting hall and couldn't see Acorn scrunching her nose up in disgust and horror.

In the end, and after a lot of poor animals had to find various ways to pretend they liked spiced fish cocoa, the penguins approved the business proposal and offered Captain Acorn the traditional business pebble to take back to the otters as a sign of the agreement. As the crew rowed back to the ship, with Acorn still insisting on standing dramatically in the front, there was a sort of happiness in the boat that only comes from seeing something challenging through to the end. Acorn felt pleased that she had managed to save the inter-action with the penguins and gave the booklet in her pocket an appreciative little pat. The crew were all proud of themselves for drinking so much cocoa without complaining, although they all looked a little sick to their stomachs and more than one animal let out a very fishy burp. The disgraced Jacob Crockey sat sullenly in the boat with no one talking to him and talking to no one himself for the rest of the day. In his mind, he had been horribly misused and ill-treated by not only the penguins, but his crew mates and captain as well. Which just goes to show that if you're having a bad attitude about something, it colors the whole way you see the world and not in a pleasant way.

I hate to say it, but Crockey didn't undergo some personality altering change that suddenly made him a nice crocodile to be around. It's rather unfortunate too because crocodiles can be lovely creatures. The four sisters had another crocodile stuffed animal who was a very polite reptile, but ones like Crockey tend to give the rest a very bad reputation. That's just the reality of things sometimes, though, and was something Captain Acorn had learned to accept. You won't always have an impact on someone that changes them for the better. Most of those times the benefit you take away from that interaction is how well you handle the situation. Sailors like Crockey would leave Captain Acorn's crew just as grumpy as they had joined it, but Acorn always felt that she had become a better squirrel each time for not letting it steal her joy.

CHAPTER SEVEN
CAPTAIN ACORN GETS A SCARE

As I've said before, there were a few things that Captain Acorn absolutely hated. She absolutely hated being ignored or made to look insignificant, and she truly despised being doubted or having someone second guess her. Both of these things, most animals knew well and did their best to avoid. There is, however, another thing that Captain Acorn absolutely hated, and that was getting scared.

I'm not, of course, referring to frightening adventures. Captain Acorn may have felt a very healthy amount of fear when her crew took on the sea serpent or battled their way through the storm, but it was a thrilling sort of fear for her. You see, part of Acorn's love of adventures was very closely tied to how scary they might be and how she might face that fear. She was perfectly fine with a little bit of scare in her adventures because she thought they helped her become a braver squirrel.

The type of being scared I mean is that sudden type of scare that makes your stomach do a somersault and your heart jump into your throat at every little sound. Acorn could fight an angry sea monster all day long, but if you asked her to take something down to a dark and creaky basement where something might make a noise at any minute, you would find yourself with a very nervous squirrel whose paws got very sweaty and whose whiskers would twitch nervously.

If Captain Acorn hated getting scared like this, she hated having people know about it even more. Her best approach for handling this secret was to charge right into it every time it came around. Any dark cave her crew uncovered was explored first by her, any strange sound in the night was quickly investigated by Acorn herself. She even somehow always found a way to know if someone was throwing her a surprise party so when the moment came she only had to throw her paws back in surprise and pretend to be scared. So no one, including Pounce, really knew that Acorn could be scared by sudden surprises and hated it.

One night, this proved to be a bit of a problem for Acorn and in many ways, she learned a bit of a lesson. They had been at sea for about a week after meeting with the penguins and so far they hadn't spotted any land or trouble. Things were going as well as they might have been expected to go. After a long day of drilling the crew on their overall preparedness for any type of emergency, Acorn had decided they had done enough work for one day and almost everyone was released to have some free time.

After spending more than a little while consulting her charts in her cabin, Acorn decided it was really time she had some free time as well. Opening the door to her cabin she called on the first crew member she saw, which happened to be Bunnerton.

"Bunnerton," she said. The rabbit in question had been walking by with a plate of cookies she had just baked and almost dropped the plate in her surprise at being addressed so suddenly "If you would be so kind as to send Pounce to my cabin, I would greatly appreciate it."

"Yes, Captain!" Bunnerton replied and turned to go, walking a little more carefully with her plate of cookies.

"Oh! And Bunnerton?"

Bunnerton's ears twitched straight up as she turned back to Acorn and said "Yes Captain?"

"May I have one of those cookies? They look divine."

Bunnerton smiled widely and was so excited to have her cookies described as divine that she hardly minded that it meant there would be one less for her.

She quickly offered one to her captain and then hurried off to find Pounce, after first dropping the cookies off in her hammock so that no one else could figure out how divine they were.

A few minutes later Pounce came eagerly bouncing into Acorn's cabin, excited as ever that something was happening, always believing it was something good first and only disappointed if it turned out to be something else entirely. In this case, Pounce's excitement was rewarded by what Acorn called her in for.

"Pounce!" She said a little secretly because that made it much more fun for the two of them. "I want to have a movie night. Why don't you run out to the movie shelf and pick one out for the two of us while I get started on some popcorn and other treats?"

If Pounce had been excited by the idea of anything general, it was nothing compared to how excited she was to have been invited to a movie night for just the two of them. She bounced and twirled excitedly around the room all while talking incredibly fast about how great this was going to be. In fact, she was so excited to get started on their movie night that she found it almost impossible to stop being excited and actually start. She kept bouncing and jabbering until eventually, Acorn managed to herd the excited cat out the door and on her way. By the time Pounce came bouncing back in her pajamas and holding a movie in her paws, Captain Acorn had made an amazingly comfy corner by her tv, complete with blankets and stuffed animals and carefully prepared snacks. Acorn prided her squirrel heritage in helping her make incredibly cozy spaces and might have been showing off a little bit.

"Ta da!" Pounce yelled as she bounced around the cabin and held the movie out for Acorn to set up. "It's that new movie that just came out, the one that's supposed to be super scary. I was looking at the movie shelf and I realized you and I have watched a lot of different kinds of movies when you've picked them, but we've never watched a scary one. So since you were having me pick this time I thought why not try a scary movie for a change? How bad can it be, really?"

Acorn gulped and thought to herself that it could be very very bad, but Pounce had already picked the movie and it seemed like there was no way out of it.

"Besides," she thought, "I'm Captain Acorn after all, what's a little scary movie compared to all the brave things I've done?" But she couldn't quite answer the question because she wasn't really convinced by what she was telling herself. So they both settled down into the cozy spot.

I don't know exactly what the movie Pounce picked was about, but I do know that it was far scarier than even Acorn had imagined it could be. The first time something scary jumped out, Acorn had to bite her lip to keep herself from squeaking in terror which she told herself would be a very undignified thing for a sea captain to do. The second time there was a big scare, Acorn jumped and knocked over the bowl of popcorn. Fortunately, she was able to blame it on Pounce, who had jumped at the same time. Acorn claimed she had only jumped to try to stop the spill from happening. The longer the movie went, the harder Acorn found it to not be afraid and not jump at the slightest noise.

"Oh thank heavens!" Acorn thought when the screen finally went black and the movie was over. She realized she was holding one of the blankets up to her chin in her tightly clenched paws and she tried to relax them as she turned to Pounce.

Pounce looked absolutely fine. Ordinarily, Acorn would have felt a little bit of pride that her First Mate was being so fearless, but that was always in situations when Acorn herself was feeling fearless and the whole thing felt a little more balanced. This time it just felt strange, confusing, and out of place. For her part, Pounce bounced up from the blankets.

"Well, that was scary!" Pounce said, although she didn't exactly look like she really meant it. True, she was still wrapped up in a blanket all the way over her head and down to the floor, but she felt perfectly fine. She moved to leave the cabin and Acorn suddenly felt that it would be a much better idea to have two of them in the cabin that night.

"Pounce!" She called, "What was that one….. Thing…. In the movie… with the…. Thing…" Acorn felt that maybe she should have thought of something to say before she started saying it. Fortunately for her, Pounce wasn't a very clever cat, and didn't suspect that Acorn was only playing for time.

"The actress?"

"No," said Acorn slowly, "the other thing."

"The actor?"

"No, not him."

"The little red bouncy ball that kept showing up in random scenes? I noticed that too, you know. Couldn't figure out why it was there though. Seemed strange to me."

Acorn jumped on the opportunity and said "Wasn't it? I mean, what was it there for?"

But Pounce ultimately disappointed her by shrugging her shoulders as she turned to go again, saying: "Dunno, Captain."

Pounce was almost to the doorway. Acorn tried again. "You know," she said slowly, "It is sort of late, and dark, and I'm sure you're very tired. Maybe you should just camp out in here with me? You know, because you must be very tired. Yes, I'm sure you're tired."

Pounce considered this for a moment before shrugging and shaking her head happily, "No thanks, Captain. I'm feeling just fine. I might go for a walk on deck before bed, come to think of it."

"Very good." Acorn sighed, giving up at last. She admired Pounce's plucky spirit and wondered if maybe being as excitable as Pounce was the key for not getting scared so easily. "Good night, Pounce. Please turn off the light as you go."

Pounce flipped the light switch off as she called out a cheerful "Goodnight!" and closed the door behind her. Acorn was now completely alone in her incredibly dark cabin. She couldn't help but wonder if her cabin had always been this dark or if this was a very new development. She tried to think back to other nights to compare the darkness of each one, but noises kept getting inside her head and pushing all other thoughts out. There seemed to be a lot of noises in that particular night. One was creaking. All through her cabin she could hear creaking that almost sounded like someone walking back and forth.

"It's just the ship, though," She told herself firmly. "If anyone actually *was* outside the door and they actually *were* scary, they wouldn't pace in front of my door a bunch of times just to get me scared before they actually started scaring me. They would come straight in. That would be the most efficient and practical way to scare an animal. Anything else would be bad technique. So it can't be anyone out there waiting to scare me."

Having decided this, Acorn snuggled deeper into her covers, feeling that she could now sleep since she had solved the mystery of the creaking. The creaking kept creaking, though, and soon it was hard to ignore.

"Has my ship always creaked this much?" she wondered as the wood made scary groaning noises in the night. "I'll have to ask Mr. Crockey to see to that first thing in the morning. That's just no good."

She tried to sleep again, but suddenly she heard a soft "swish swish" noise that sounded like her blanket brushing against the floor.

"It's all right!" she told herself sternly, "the ship must just be rocking your bed in a way that's making the blanket brush over the floor. If something scary was in my room, I don't think it would get so easily distracted by swishing a blanket over the floor. Not when it has important scaring stuff to do."

She pulled the blanket all the way up to her chin, but as the ship rocked on the ocean the blanket kept swishing on the floor. It always seems to be the case that when you don't want to think about something, that suddenly becomes the thing you think about most. For Captain Acorn, that thing became monsters.

She started to wonder if there was any way a monster could have gotten aboard the Golden Acorn, and if it had she wondered if she was fully prepared and ready to face it. Acorn suddenly found herself wishing that she had had some sort of Monster Preparedness Plan. It seemed like a really good idea to have one in place because you never know when a monster will decide to make itself known. So she started thinking of a plan as quick as she could to fix the fact that she didn't already have one.

The first step of her Monster Preparedness Plan, or MPP as she started calling it, was to make sure you had a kit for it. She carefully got out of bed, turned on the light (and then, of course, looked around frantically to make sure a monster wasn't taking advantage of her not already having an MPP), and pulled a small box off one of her shelves. In it, she carefully placed her second best captain's pistol, a flashlight, and a net for first trapping a monster.

Pleased with the success of the first step, Acorn decided that the second step would be making a search of the entire area to make sure no monsters were present, which would lead to the third step of the MPP: getting a good night's sleep because you were very prepared. Tucking the box under her arm, she cautiously opened the door to her cabin and peered out into the night. No monsters were present.

Feeling a little encouraged, she continued the search below deck. With each area she deemed "monster free" she felt braver and braver until suddenly she heard a noise on the deck above her: footsteps. Acorn's heart started thumping hard in her chest and her paws got very sweaty. She suddenly felt very torn between running back to her cabin and facing the monster on deck.

"This is the problem with an MPP," she told herself in a very squeaky voice, "You spend too much time preparing for a monster and then you don't have a Monster on Deck Plan."

Acorn was a very miserable and scared squirrel, but she hoped that maybe she would be able to come up with a Monster on Deck Plan once she was up there, so she carefully climbed on deck and looked around. The monster was still walking around and Acorn could hear the footsteps going this way and that way in the dark. Still, she didn't know exactly where the monster was and that made her start to shake a little because she knew that monsters probably liked to jump out and scare squirrels before they attacked.

"Monster?" Acorn tried to ask bravely, but instead, her voice came out very squeaky and scared.

The monster footsteps came closer, but Acorn couldn't quite tell which way they were coming from. She held onto the MPP box even tighter, but because she was so scared she never even thought to try opening it up and using it, which would have only helped her feel a little braver. Unfortunately, when we are scared we rarely think straight until after and then we come up with plans for how we could have done things differently. Suddenly, the monster was right behind Acorn and put its monster paw right on her shoulder.

"AUGH!!!" Screamed Acorn in her squeakiest voice yet, "Back! Get back monster! Please don't hurt me! I mean, no! Fear me! Fear me monster!"

"Captain?" said the monster in a much smaller voice than monsters typically have, "Are you all right?"

Captain Acorn went from being a very scared squirrel to being a very embarrassed squirrel as she realized that the monster was actually just Pounce. Turning around she saw her First Mate standing on deck, looking very confused and worried about her captain.

"Pounce!" Acorn tried to yell happily as if nothing was wrong, but her voice came out a little shaky because the rest of her was shaking even worse. "Pounce! It's just Pounce! Good old Pounce!"

Pounce was a little flattered by the very sudden praise, but was still very confused by how Acorn was acting. So she asked: "Are you ok, Captain?"

Acorn laughed a little too hard and cleared her throat before saying "Totally ok! Thanks for asking, Pounce!"

"I didn't scare you, did I?"

"Pffft!" Captain Acorn blustered, "No! Scare me? No way! What would make you think a thing like that?"

She and Pounce looked at each other for a long, quiet moment before Acorn said in a much smaller voice: "Don't tell the others?"

Pounced gave a little wink.

"Not a word."

Acorn nodded and clapped her paws together. "Excellent! Well, uh, I think I'll be going then."

"What were you doing out here, Captain?" Pounce asked, "I thought you had gone to bed."

"Nothing," Replied Acorn briskly, "Nothing at all, just making sure the MPP was in ship shape."

She quickly hurried off to her room and back to bed, leaving Pounce alone on the deck to wonder what exactly an MPP was and why her Captain needed to be sure it was in ship shape.

CHAPTER EIGHT
CAPTAIN ACORN HAS A BATTLE

The sailing had been going quite well for several weeks without any trouble in sight. The disappointing thing about that sort of atmosphere is that when trouble does strike, it is very unexpected and tends to hurt a little worse because of it. Trouble arrived quite suddenly for the crew and Captain of the Golden Acorn, and it was mostly Acorn's fault, but she would never have openly admitted it.

Captain Acorn liked to think that she was a very observant squirrel, but there's a very big difference between thinking you are something and actually being something. In this instance, Acorn was not at all an observant squirrel. It was a late afternoon when the sun was just starting to set across the sea and Acorn had volunteered to keep watch. In her mind it was a chance to work alongside her crew and deepen their respect for her, so she did it with some frequency.

High up the mast of the ship, she perched quietly, keeping her gaze scanning across the horizon. From her great height, it was easy to start talking to herself and once she did that she found there was praise due. After all, on this voyage alone she had hauled an enormous treasure off of the sea floor with the help of Pounce, and the crew was all going to be given huge bonuses, which would only boost her image as a captain. She had also defeated a sea serpent (which was a first) and successfully handled a diplomatic mission. Few captains at her age had so much success in their entire careers, let alone a single voyage. Although she reminded herself modestly, it wouldn't be very good for her to let that go to her head. A good captain was always humble, no matter how great and brave they were.

While she sat there thinking about the balance between being proud of herself and being humble, and just how much of that actually needed to be humility, she suddenly got a very real reminder on how important it really is to be humble. If she hadn't been giving so much thought to how great she was, she might have seen the ship coming over the horizon a little sooner, and she would have seen the angry looking flag flapping in the breeze from its mast. It wasn't until they fired their first cannon and it made a tremendous splash in the water next to the Golden Acorn that Acorn realized they were in danger of an attack

"Enemies ahead!" she cried from her perch, and then she slid down a rope to the deck and began giving more orders.

Most of the crew had figured out that enemies were ahead after the splash from the cannonball in the water, but they respected Acorn too much to bring that up, so instead they all began hurrying around to carry out her orders for battle. Within minutes, the entire crew had swords and pistols out and the cannon team was firing back at the strange ship and the several other crew members were dealing with ropes and sails while Pounce shouted orders. Captain Acorn pulled out her spyglass and looked out across the water. When she got a closer look at the enemy ship she gave as fierce of a growl as a squirrel her size could manage.

"Pounce!" she called, "It's the hamsters!"

The crew, who all heard her shout to Pounce, all made their own loud, angry noises which made quite a commotion since a lot of different animals were present and they all had very different ways of expressing their anger. Even though it had been months since the Gala on Bunny Island, the crew of the Golden Acorn hadn't easily forgotten their dislike of the hamster crew and their captain Hamsterton, especially Acorn.

She stalked angrily up to the helm of the ship where Pounce was hard at work. Acorn's whiskers were twitching wildly with rage and her nose was scrunching more and more in disgust at their opponents.

"I don't understand it, Pounce." Captain Acorn said frostily, "A snub isn't worth an attack like this."

Pounce, who had been staring straight ahead and looking almost as furious as her captain, suddenly looked very intensely at her paws at the helm and Acorn became suspicious at once.

"Pounce," she said slowly, "This is just about what I said to them at the party isn't it?"

Pounce nodded quickly.

"Pounce."

Pounce shook her head quickly.

Acorn sighed loudly in frustration well deserved. "Pounce! What did you do?"

"I uh- I," stammered the nervous cat, "I may have- uh- left them a cake by their boat."

This was not at all what Captain Acorn was expecting to hear and she suddenly felt very confused why hamsters would start a naval battle over a cake. Pounce had a marvelous taste in cakes, so it couldn't possibly be that it wasn't tasty. She tried a new line of questioning.

"Were there any words in the frosting?"

Pounce became even more focused on her paws and Captain Acorn pressed her further.

"Pounce, as your captain, I order you to tell me what frosting writing you put on that cake."

"It was- uh-" Pounce squeaked nervously, "That is, it said…. 'Smooth sailing, hamsters! Acorn out!'"

Acorn ran her paws over her face and sighed again. "Honestly, Pounce," she said, "That was your big idea? You wrote an insult on a cake? A cake?

Everyone likes cake Pounce! How is it teaching them a lesson if you give them something tasty?"

"It does seem rather foolish now that I look back on it, Captain." Pounce replied humbly. "Although, it does seem that they still took the insult since they're trying to attack us now."

"That's not a good thing," Acorn said, pinching the bridge of her nose and trying to be calmer than she ever had been before. Squirrels aren't known for keeping their cool, so Captain Acorn being not just calm but very calm was an extraordinary thing. Still, I suppose you don't get to Captain Acorn's place in life by losing your cool, so you have to find little tricks to keep it all together.

There was no more time now to discuss how effective the cake had been in insulting the hamsters, though, because they had nearly caught up to the Golden Acorn.

"Get ready, crew!" Captain Acorn yelled fiercely. She drew her sword and pointed it in the direction of the enemy ship as it came alongside them. "Show these hamsters that the Golden Acorn will not be so easily taken!

The crew all cheered wildly, but it was less because they were excited and more because they weren't. They were all doing a very smart thing which is choosing an emotion to have before an emotion chooses you. They all felt a little afraid, but each of them wanted to be brave more than anything, so that's what they chose to be. Acorn would have felt a little afraid as she waited for the hamsters to start the fighting, but she kept the fear away by remembering all the other battles she had been in and wondering where this one would rank in her favorites after it was all said and done.

In a matter of moments, the hamsters had pulled alongside the Golden Acorn. Their ship was significantly smaller and less impressive which gave Acorn a brief feeling of superiority. But where it lacked in size, it made up for ferocity. The deck was crowded with angry, round hamsters who were all armed to the teeth and squeaking furious battle cries at Acorn and her crew. At the helm of the ship, very much mirroring Acorn's own stance, was Hamsterton and another hamster who was presumably his first mate. Hamsterton glowered at Acorn as their eyes met across the narrow space of water between them and he shook his paw and yelled something at her that she couldn't quite understand. She assumed it was something unflattering and she was very right to guess so. Choosing to ignore his insults, Acorn raised her sword aloft and let loose with her shrillest, squeakiest battle cry and her entire crew followed, bellowing, chirping, hissing, and squeaking their challenges.

The battle erupted into noises of "pew pew!" and "boom!" as Captain Acorn's faithful crew went to war against the hamsters. Once or twice the battle got so intense that the adults in the front seat had to remind the sisters not to get too loud while they were driving. Whenever this happened, the battle turned into more of a stealth operation, with each side probing the weaknesses of the other and hoping to find a way to overpower them.

It was during one of these moments that the hamsters almost won the battle, which would have been a serious blow to Captain Acorn's self-esteem. It's probably for that very reason that Hamsterton and his crew attacked the Golden Acorn in the first place. I doubt that they knew about the treasure, and I don't think they wanted the ship for themselves. Hamsterton seemed to believe that if he couldn't make the seafaring world respect him by his words, he was going to make them do so by his actions. The ridiculous part of this was that almost everyone but Hamsterton knew that reputations are earned not demanded. It only made him look more ridiculous and small-minded that he thought he was doing something never seen before.

In a desperate move to earn his reputation on the sea, Hamsterton ordered some of his crew to load the biggest, but quietest (because the sisters didn't want to get in trouble for making unexpected noises) cannon and aim it right at the bow of the ship where Pounce was standing and brandishing her sword. Some of his fellow hamsters were confused why he was pointing the cannon at anyone less important than Acorn herself. The truth is that this was one occasion where Hamsterton was being very clever. He knew Acorn was on full alert and angrily watching every move he made, so to point the cannon at her would give her more than enough time to react. Point it at someone who wasn't known for paying attention, though, and Hamsterton believed he had a chance at Captain Acorn.

Hamsterton's fatal mistake was the same mistake he made he'd made before: he overestimated himself and underestimated Captain Acorn. Just as he gave the order to fire (in an appropriate inside voice of course), Captain Acorn swung in a wide semicircle from her ship. With a shrill battle cry, she kicked the cannon sideways so hard that it spun around completely to face Hamsterton right as it went off.

Hamsterton was naturally very shocked to suddenly be face to face with a cannon that he had just ordered to fire in the opposite direction. He ducked down as quickly as he could and the cannon went off with a tremendous (but appropriately quiet) "BANG!". For as quick as he had tried to be, Hamsterton wasn't quite quick enough. The cannonball sailed off into the distance, but not before it had singed all the fur on the top of his head in a neat stripe.

At first, Hamsterton didn't even realize what had happened, but all his crew had turned to him in horror, staring at the top of his head instead of straight at him. He reached up nervously and patted the area with his paw. Realizing what had happened, Hamsterton let out a little wail of complete and total embarrassment and tried to cover what had happened by frantically grabbing the nearest hamster's hat, which happened to be a very large, napoleonic looking hat. The damage was already done, though. His entire crew – and a large number of the Golden Acorn's crew – had seen what had happened and were either laughing or trying their hardest not to laugh.

To make matters worse for the hamsters and better for the Golden Acorn, the incident with the cannonball had distracted the hamsters long enough that before they knew it the crew of the Golden Acorn had swarmed onto their ship

and the whole battle was over. The Hamsters all threw down their weapons and put their hands up. All except for Hamsterton who was holding on tightly to his newly acquired hat and looking more embarrassed than any hamster had ever looked before.

Into the middle of this surrender strode Captain Acorn. She had slid down the rope she'd been swinging on and had landed nimbly and silently in the midst of her crew. They all looked at her expectantly and she thrust her sword in the air and yelled:

"Animals of the Golden Acorn! Victory is ours!"

Everyone cheered loudly and hugged, being careful to not poke each other with swords, harpoons, and other weapons as they did. The hamsters, of course, didn't join in any of the cheering and glared sullenly at Captain Acorn. She didn't care in the slightest, though, and walked straight up to where Hamsterton was still clutching his hat. The embarrassed hamster glared at her furiously, but lowered one hand from his hat to offer her his sword as an act of surrender.

"Captain Acorn," He said stiffly, "You have bested me in battle. My ship is yours."

To Hamsterton's credit, he was a sullen loser, but not a completely ungracious one. He knew that being defeated in battle meant Acorn could take his ship if she wanted to and he wasn't putting up any sort of whiny fuss. He was taking it in stride.

Acorn took the sword from him and examined it. It was a beautifully crafted sword with Hamsterton's initials engraved on the hilt. From the way it gleamed in the sunlight, it was clear that he took great care of it, same as Acorn would take care of her own sword. Looking around his ship, she could see that he took care of his ship just as well as his sword. Besides some mess from the battle, things were neat and orderly, showing the Captain's pride in them.

Even though it was her right as the Captain of the winning ship, Acorn didn't like the idea of taking Hamsterton's ship from him. In her mind, no animal deserved to be denied the sea, even if it was a self-important hamster who couldn't take a joke. She decided to be merciful. Well, mostly merciful.

"I'll tell you what, Hamsterton," Acorn went on with a mischievous grin, "I won't keep your ship. You can set sail from here with your entire crew. All I want is a small token of my victory here."

Hamsterton looked completely shocked at this turn of events, but he quickly nodded to accept her terms and gestured to the sword.

"You are too kind," he said with forced humility, "Please, keep it."

Acorn smiled and shook her head. "No, no. I won't take your sword. I would very much like your hat, though."

Hamsterton's whiskers froze nervously and his paws gripped the hat a little tighter. A few members of Captain Acorn's crew had to cover their mouths with paws or wings to cover laughter.

"I'd really rather you took the ship," Hamsterton said nervously.

Acorn leaned in a little closer and smiled a little wider. Even though she was smiling, her eyes made it abundantly clear that Hamsterton shouldn't test her any further.

"All the same, Hamsterton, the hat please."

Shaking with embarrassment and anger, Hamsterton slowly reached up and removed his hat, handing it to Acorn. She turned it over in her hands a few times and then placed it on her head with a smug grin. The Golden Acorn crew all started trying a lot harder not to laugh and the hamsters all let out little groans and sighs of embarrassment.

Acorn was certainly rubbing it in, but that's fairly understandable considering Hamsterton had by this point insulted her at a formal event, attacked her ship for no other reason than he couldn't take a joke, and had tried to personally blast her first mate with a cannon. There wasn't much chance of him gaining sympathy with anyone but his fellow hamsters.

For his part, Hamsterton was trying his best to look dignified, but that's an incredibly hard thing to do when you've just been defeated in a sea battle and are missing a large strip of fur along the top of your head. He pointed his nose high in the air (which only made the sun glint on the bald patch more), nodded stuffily to Acorn, and strode away with his crew following sulkily. After watching him go for a moment, Acorn turned to her crew, and raised the hat in salute with a cheeky grin. That was the final straw for the crew, and they all laughed uncontrollably as they crossed back over to Golden Acorn and sailed away from the disgraced hamsters.

For the rest of the day, Acorn scanned the horizon intensely, still wearing the hat, but no more trouble came. The crew went about their work, but was continuously distracted by the image of their captain standing boldly and wearing her prized hat. She looked regal enough, but the reality was that she was determined to not let anything else catch her by surprise for the remainder of the voyage.

As for Pounce, she never found out that Captain Acorn had saved her from being blasted across the sea by a cannonball. Acorn may have liked being praised and looked up to, but she had her moments when she knew it was better to keep quiet about a good deed and simply enjoy that she had been able to do it. This was one of those moments. Acorn was perfectly content to know what she had done and it made her smile with relief to know that her clumsy, loyal, awkward, dear first mate was still sailing with her at the end of the day.

CHAPTER NINE
CAPTAIN ACORN'S ADVENTURES COME TO A CLOSE

The four sisters could have easily kept spinning so many more fantastic stories of Acorn and Pounce and Bunnerton and Froglen and Crockey (and they later did). For the time being, though, the adventures had to end because the parents in the front seat had given them a fifteen-minute warning before they arrived and the sisters all knew that the time had come to end this particular voyage of their fantastic, seafaring squirrel.

For this adventure, the end came with the buildings of Old Harbor, and the mountains behind them, slowly coming into view on the horizon as the Golden Acorn glided over the last few miles of calm sea on her way home in the light of a golden sunset. The majority of the crew was cheering and whooping, giving each other high fives and warmly shaking each other's paws to congratulate each other on completing the voyage. They talked excitedly of how they were going to set themselves up for life with their pay from the voyage, or how they planned to audition for another of Acorn's crews, or wondered if they would be more popular by association with the famous squirrel. Crockey even joined the conversation, but only to grumpily announce that no one would ever catch him setting sail again. The chatter went back and forth across the ship as it drew closer to the harbor, but not all the animals on board were taking part.

For a small number of the crew, seeing the end of their adventure so near turned them into very thoughtful animals. It's perfectly normal to feel this way. Sometimes the best way to celebrate something is by reflecting warmly on it.

For Bunnerton, this meant finishing up a journal entry on the whole experience and baking one last batch of cookies, this time for the whole crew. Mousell lay in his hammock and flipped through the various pictures he had taken on the voyage, most of which were partially obscured by his paws because he wasn't a very good photographer. Pounce stood at the helm, still on duty, but sighing so contentedly that she may have accidentally had a lapse of attention and briefly set the ship off course.

Acorn herself was perched high up in the lookout. Besides going up there to reflect on herself, it was an excellent place to take some quiet moments and consider the work she did. As the Golden Acorn sliced through the sparkling sunset waters, she felt that same tug she always did when seeing Old Harbor coming into view: the tug to do it all again. She was already eagerly calculating the time it would take to audition a new crew and set sail again. Yes, she would be back out on the sea in no time with a new crew of eager young animals to show the ways of seafaring.

In many ways, and although Acorn would never admit to anyone (not even herself) the greatest thing she ever took away from one of her voyages was the change in her crew. She loved to see each one of them as they came back to port, looking out over the water, and thought of all the ways they had grown and changed in the months of their sailing. Adventures, treasure, and fame or not, as long as these animals came back a little braver than before, she was happy.

With a happy sigh, Acorn grabbed a nearby rope and slid neatly down to land next to Pounce, who stood up straight and tried to look like she hadn't just been off course. Acorn knew she had, but decided that this wasn't the time to bring it up. Without a word, she gave Pounce's shoulder and affectionate pat and went back to staring over the water.

"Was it a good voyage, Captain?" Pounce asked as they neared the harbor.

Captain Acorn smiled at her First Mate warmly. "It was a very good voyage, my friend. One of the best."

"Good," Pounce said, now smiling as well. "I was hoping you thought so too."

And so Captain Acorn's voyage came to an end and the crew all disembarked. But that wouldn't be the last voyage of the Golden Acorn. For as long as there were four girls on a car ride with a stuffed squirrel handy, there was always the chance for another adventure.

ABOUT THE AUTHOR

Avalon Robinson shared her first short story at a student showcase when she was nine and has been hooked on writing ever since. *The Fantastic Adventures of Captain Acorn* is her first book. She has a degree in history from the University of Idaho and lives in North Idaho. You can find her on Instagram or online at avalonrobinson.com

CPSIA information can be obtained
at www.ICGtesting.com
Printed in the USA
FSHW011113180219
55749FS